Hoi

♦

Pan Panziarka

v e l v e t

HOUSE OF PAIN
Pan Panziarka
ISBN 1 871592 57 7
A Velvet Book
Copyright © Pan Panziarka 1995
First edition 1995
Reprinted 1997
Copyright © Velvet Publicationss 1997
All rights reserved
Published by
VELVET PUBLICATIONS
83 Clerkenwell Road
London EC1, UK
Tel: 0171-430-9878
Fax: 0171-242-5527
A Bondagebest Production
♦
Design:
Bradley Davis, PCP International

This book is dedicated to Gina Pantziarka, whose cancer death at the age of 29 caused such unbearable pain and suffering to all who loved her. She didn't deserve to die, and when she did the best part of me went with her.

The pain of her death served to remind me of a truth I had been stupid enough to forget—

The universe doesn't give a fuck

ONE

The car is black. As though it can be any other colour. Black, sleek, phallic. Glistening with a thousand jewels of light as I stand in the pouring rain. Monochrome vision. Black leather skirt against my white flesh, black leather jacket and tightly buttoned waistcoat. Black ankle boots with half a dozen straps to keep even the fussiest boot queen happy. White face, drained of colour and emotion. Bloodless apart from the bright, glossy stuff on my lips, fake bloodied red to turn my mouth into an oozing pussy waiting to be filled.

I wait, bored out of my skull, limbs icy and aching. Long black car, smoothing to a standstill at the kerb. Moments earlier I had been caught in the beams of light, stereophonic beacons that caught the rain and held the light mid-stream. Flash lights for a flash car, I wonder what kind of sad bastard has a car this good and is still reducing to crawling the streets looking for some pussy. What kind of limp dick am I going to be offered?

I wait. Back against the wall, the rain sluicing down my leathers, rivulets that dazzle as I watched. Wet, I like that, I like being wet and slutty and out on the street when every other whore is either giving head or junked out of her brain. I like it and that worries me. It worries the fuck out of me.

The car purrs a feline sound that matches the hiss of the rain on the pavement. The windows are misted over but I can sense two bodies waiting for me. Rich bastard and his driver, it has to be. What does he want? Poor little poor girl? Wretched jail bait? Junked out whore? Sleazy bitch? What fucking game is he going to ask for? Fat jaded bastard, whacked out over his wanking fantasies just so's he can could get a few inches of dick to go semi-hard. Does he want me to suck it, bite it, lick it, swallow it, fuck it, take it up the ass, in my cunt, in my mouth?

Electric window glides down smoothly, just the way the car glided to a halt in front of me. Dark inside the car. Always is. Dark, just like the miserable fucking night. And then the face appears. Pale skin, lips as red as my own, dark eyes and black hair. She half smiles, a quiver of her lips and a sparkle in those eyes. I swallow hard, boredom flushed away with the rain that seems to fall harder.

I step forward, wishing I had a cigarette to stamp out with the steel tipped heels of my boots, grinding it down the way I'd grind down a man's prick. The sharp rhythm of high heels on granite sounds good though, a cheap thrill that never does business any harm. My face is blank, ruby lips set hard, giving every impression that I am still fucking bored out of my tiny mind.

Framed by the car window, her face is beautiful, tiny lines around the eyes and mouth making her look more human than me. The bitch looks good, her eyes shining with curiosity as she watches me walk the half dozen steps towards her. I try to look past her, but the inside of the car is obscured. Dark but warm, a place to hide from the miserable drizzle that lands sweat all over me. There is a driver up front, a vague shadow that I can just about make out. Not that I'm interested in him.

She is sizing me up, eyes scanning the skinny little whore in front of her. Is she really interested? Fuck. I've never done it with a woman for money. All I ever get are dirty male specimens who come in their pants as soon as I wiggle my backside at them. I'm sick of that, sick of the taste of sour spunk and unwashed prick. What would she want? What would she have me do?

'Nice car,' I say, voice hovering between little girl innocent and dirty tart. Most johns want my baby voice, they like the idea of fucking little girls no bigger than their daughters.

'I like you,' she replies, her facing finally finishing the smile she's been toying with. Nice white teeth against red lips, nice, expensive teeth. Good breeding and an accent that only money and education can buy.

'I like you, too,' I reply, allowing myself a smile. I mean it. Whore with a heart of gold, shit. I'm looking forward to getting out of the rain, into her knickers and then into her purse.

She slides back from the window, pushing her body along the squeaky clean leather seats. The door is open to the enticing warmth. I am enveloped by that warmth, perfumed expensively. You just know that it takes the guts of animals to manufacture that scent. The rain is still falling, relentlessly, grinding down and sucking away any resolve I might have had. I am alone, the only girl on the street stupid enough to wait at this time of the night and in this shitty weather. Even the bitches owned by the meanest pimps are safely out of the way.

What fucking difference does it make? Witnesses or not, I'm fucking desperate and this bitch in the car looks like she's just landed from planet cash. It has to be black, this car, it can't be anything else. Even the interior is dark, warm, bodily. A nice inviting snatch of a car, there is no way I can resist. One moment I am there, spiked heels standing my corner, a leather clad slut and the next I am safely cosseted, a passenger for the night.

Pressed back into the soft leather seat by the sudden acceleration, I let myself go. Breathing in that expensive scent which perfumes her body, an aura that wraps her and traps me. She is beside me, laughing softly, happy that I am with her. Soft hands, long painted nails manicured with precision, her warm fingers stroking my arm.

I am freezing. Icy flesh white and bloodless, beautifully cadaverous. I could play dead and she can fuck me back to life if she wants. I'd keep quiet, eyes closed, body still, the fluids leaking from my cunt into her mouth until I orgasm to life again. Reborn.

'How old are you?' she asks, leaning back, her hand resting on mine.

Standard question. 'How old do you want me to be?' I ask in return. Standard response. They all have an age in mind, some precisely worked combination of years and months that triggers their libido. Fuck knows how, this is numerology gone haywire, every combination of digits pumping blood into someone's prick. Only this time it's a woman doing the asking. Does it work that way for her too, her cunt running wet with delight when the numbers trip from my lips?

She purses her lips for a moment, thinking. Sexy move. I bet she's worked that trick down to a tee. 'Take three years off your real age,' she suggests.

'I'm fourteen,' I tell her.

'Let's make you thirteen,' she decides, smiling again.

'I'm thirteen,' I agree. It's part of the script now, I'm going to be thirteen for however long she pays me.

She is dressed in red. Short skirt and bare legs, red high heels,

Pan Panziarka

red jacket and top. Black car and red clothes. Colour co-ordinated, black and red, primal, anarchist colours. Black and red, Nazi colours too, imbued with authority. Long legs. I like that. Smooth thighs, well shaped, high heels that give her power even though she is sitting sideways on the seat. This fucking bitch looks real good. Any fucker that can buy her can buy a hundred like me.

'You're cold,' she tells me, rubbing her long fingers against my thigh.

I am afraid to get too close, scared that I'm going to get her all wet and cold, that my body will pour second hand rain all over her. Soft fingers sliding up and down my thigh, sensuously, deliciously. I close my eyes to enjoy the sensation, her fingers against the cool wetness of my thighs, joining up the dots of rain like jism against my skin. The warmth and the touch of her fingers are soothing and exciting, reminders of a world that I had once imagined but never dreamed of seeing. Doesn't she want to beat me? Isn't she going to let me know that I am just some cheap piece of meat to be fucked and discarded? Why the hell is she exciting me, seducing what she's paying for?

'So cold,' she whispers, her breath sweetness itself against my lips.

I half open my eyes, exhale softly, enjoying the closeness of her body and the velvet touch of her fingers against my thigh. So good. My heart is beating, faster and faster, as though the unaccustomed warmth and sensuality signal danger.

'I'm freezing,' I whisper quietly, my child's voice making itself heard for the first time. My real voice, not some unconvincing act to make a john come quicker. Cold water drips from my hair, slipping down smoothly over my face and down onto my shiny leather jacket. I am still afraid to touch her, afraid that she'd push me away, afraid that I'd pollute her with the dirty water that bathes me.

'Come here, baby,' she says softly, opening her arms. Dark eyes watch me with a mixture of tenderness and desire, drawing me closer as I feel myself falling into her embrace.

She cuddles me, pressing my face against her chest, brushing her elegant fingers through my hair and being soaked. So warm, her flesh trembling as my lips brush against her. Arms around me protectively, her voice murmuring softly in my ear. Eyes closed and I am in heaven. The rocking of the car and the beat of her heart are all that I need.

'So cold, baby,' she repeats, kissing my face softly. Chaste kisses. Mother daughter kisses. I relax in her arms, allowing myself to slip back. Only thirteen. Only a child in her mother's arms.

'Hold me, mummy,' I whisper, aware that my thighs are pressed tightly against her long legs, her heat warming me up too.

'My baby, my baby,' she coos. More kisses, tender, loving, needy. Kisses on the forehead, the eyes, the cheek and finally, softly, barely perceptible, on the mouth. I hold my breath, hesitant, and then sigh. She kisses me again, on the mouth, her lips brushing mine, her tongue protruding slightly between my lips. Such kisses. No one has kissed me like this before. Unhurried. Sensuous. Incestuous.

I turn slightly towards her, heart pounding, excitement deep in my pussy. This isn't part of the deal. Being a whore means hating everyone I fuck. Being a whore is a mercenary sickness. Being a whore means being alone, always and without exception.

'So cold, let mummy warm you, baby,' she sighs breathily, her mouth touching my own. Her hands are on my thighs again, sliding up and down, slowly, pressing my flesh to warm it up.

My nipples are hard, first from the cold and now from desire. The bitch is turning me on. Sensitive fingers on my thighs, sneaking under the cool leather skirt to touch me more intimately. She is moving slowly, inching her fingers to the dark triangle of lace over my pussy. My sex is aching, pussy lips pressing against black lace, heat and desire oozing inside me. Bitch. Why doesn't she just take me? Why doesn't she slip her painted nails between my cunt lips, why?

'Oh, mummy,' I exclaim, shivering and shimmering. A real sigh. Not pretend. Not an act that I've put on to get it over and done with quickly. Her fingers stroking the inside of my thigh, making me squirm with excitement and want. Touch me you bitch! Fucking rip my skirt off and press your fingers into my cunt. Show me what a whore I am, fuck me mercilessly then throw the money in my face.

She sighs too, her eyes half closed and fluttering as she exhales. She is hot. 'Mummy is here, baby, mummy will look after you,' she murmurs maternally.

I try to touch her, letting my fingers rest on the softness of her thigh but she gently moves my hand away. Mummy is in charge. I am thirteen. And hot.

Buttons undone on my waistcoat, first one and then another two quickly. Her hand slides onto my chest, exploring the warmth between flesh and leather. Small breasts but hard nipples, her fingers tracing the contours of my chest and then closing over the hard point of flesh. Pressing hard until I utter a sigh of pain into her mouth, my breath sucked down as her tongue goes deeper between my lips. I'm starting to feel lost, moving into that unfamiliar territory where I have no control. My cunt is oozing, sticky wetness soiling lacy black knickers.

I try again, daring to touch her. I feel her breasts over her top, touching softly and pleased to find that her nipples are as hard as my own. She squeezes again, making me fold in her arms, drawing out my resolve as I exhale the sharp pain that I love so much.

'Oh, mummy, mummy, mummy,' I whisper deliriously. My waistcoat is undone, my breasts displayed, smooth white skin with chocolate coloured nipples, puckered hard with excitement. She is dazzled, her eyes feasting on my tits, her hands stroking and touching all the while.

'Be a good girl for mummy,' she tells me and kisses me on the mouth again.

I climax. Shuddering and gasping as her mouth crushes my own. I can hardly breath, my nipples scratched by the steel zipper on my leather jacket. She is all over me, sensuously touching and kissing and whispering. Jesus. I'm panting, delirious. I want her to fuck me. I want her to push me to the ground and finger fuck my cunt until I can take no more.

'Oh, my baby, mummy's here,' she tells me, tenderly. Kissing me again, on the face and mouth, her fingers tweaking my nipples playfully.

I've never been turned on by a paying customer, never. No matter how good looking, how expert, how perverse. Fuck it. If a man's paying for sex then he's shit, even if it's me he's paying for. Never done it with a woman before, not for real. But if she's paying for my pussy then she's shit as well. Only this fucking bitch is turning me inside out. My knickers are soaked. My tits are hard.

She takes my fingers and kisses them softly, looking directly into my eyes as she does so. I see desire there, pure animal sex, but also tenderness, curiosity. There's more but I can't fucking read it. All I know about is sex. She kisses my fingers softly, touching the very tip of her red lips to the tips of my fingers. For a moment I think she's going to suck my fingers into her mouth, or run her tongue across them or something. She takes my hand and guides it under my skirt, up between my thighs.

I offer my fingers to her. Pussy soaked. Wet with the juice from my cunt. It's hers. She's paying. She sniffs, breathes the scent of my cunt and then kisses my fingers again. 'You've wet yourself, my darling,' she informs me, gently scolding her daughter.

'I'm sorry, mummy,' I say, flooding my pussy with more juice.

She smiles understandingly. I watch as she takes her red jacket off. She's braless under her silky top. As I watch I touch myself, pressing my fingers deep into my pussy as I push aside my knickers. It feels good, waves of pleasure making me moan softly. Very slowly she undoes the buttons of her top, revealing her firm breasts, full and rounded, beautiful nipples like dark haloes.

'Come to mummy,' she sighs invitingly. She takes my hand and sucks away my emissions, tasting her daughter's cunt juices and smiling. I'm close to orgasm again.

Her nipples are perfumed, scented with the glands of animals so that I'm dizzy. I suckle, pull on the nipples that gave me nourishment as a baby. Baby's back to mummy. Her hand strokes my hair as I suck her, biting her nipples between my teeth, lashing my tongue back and forth over the fleshy bud. I hold her, glad, at last, to touch mummy. She's beautiful and sexy, sharing her body with her thirteen year old daughter.

I stroke her thighs at last, long and smooth, flawless flesh that I already adore. She is panting hard, her chest is patterned red with the flush of pleasure. I don't care any more, I don't want to think, all I want is to make love to mummy. Her skin tastes of honey and I long to sink my tongue into her pussy, to lap at her come as I make it pour from her body.

Her hand sneaks down and finds my sex. My knickers are a mess, a thin strip of lace pushed between my bulging pussy lips. Each time I move it rubs deliciously against my clit. I feel as though I've pissed myself, my thighs are wet and sticky. When her fingertip brushes against the material I shudder, moaning softly in anticipation.

'You've been good to mummy,' she says as I suck on her tits, 'now it's time to meet daddy.'

I look up, my mouth still tingling from sucking her nipples. She is smiling. Then she laughs as she sees the confusion.

She pulls her skirt up, slowly, exposing her lovely thighs, the first dark pubic hairs and then her hard cock, clothed in red silk panties. A hard rod of flesh straining against silk, a dark wet patch bleeding from the tip. Heavy balls cased in expensive lingerie. Smooth white flesh, the best legs I'd ever seen joined in the middle by a thick meaty erection.

'Now it's daddy's turn,' she tells me. He tells me. Same fucking voice, only somehow there's an edge there.

I stare. Transfixed. Such lovely breasts, beautiful nipples now ringed with my teeth marks, dripping with spit where I've been sucking them.

I'm being pushed down, off the warm leather seat. Down into the gap between the front and rear seats. On my knees. Familiar territory. Down on my fucking knees where I belong.

I suddenly panic. I don't know where the fuck I am. Lights flash past, stroboscopic effects as the car speeds along.

'Be good for daddy,' I am told, as her long, elegant fingers, still perfumed, unravel her cock from her knickers.

I kiss softly, my mouth touching the velvety softness of hard prick. But that's too good for a bitch like me. It's forced into my mouth, invading me, taking ownership at last. I don't resist, I know the score, I'm a cheap fucking whore.

'Suck for daddy, be good for daddy,' a steady incantation as a thirteen year old goes down. I'm sucking hard, moving my head up and down, the flat side of my tongue moving on the underside of his cock. His cock. Her cock. Mummy. Daddy. The whole freaking fucking family.

A slap, hard across the face. I fall back. Not doing it right. Pretty manicured nails squeeze hard on my nipples, making me cry out. Again. Mouth wrapped tightly against hard flesh. I can taste the pre-come, I can taste the perfumed body I have lost myself to.

Bitch. This is what I deserve. This is where it begins. Mummy. Daddy. Family fucking. Thirteen year old slut. Captured.

'Swallow it all.'

Thick waves of come, spunk deep into my mouth. Body jerking as I swallow. And then I'm released. On my knees, head resting against the warm leather trim, a trail of slimy spit falling from the corner of my mouth. Cock safely stashed, mummy is stroking my hair again.

'Where are we going?' I ask, finally.

A smile. Beautiful lips slightly smeared. Tenderness in her voice. I can feel her spunk sitting in my stomach, sticking to the sides of my throat.

'To oblivion,' she says.

TWO

The car glides to a halt. Darkness again. As if the light of day were ever to be allowed. My body is aching and I feel slightly sick, the way I always do after swallowing a stomach full of spunk. Some whores claim to love it, to feast on that junk from a man's prick but not me. I swallow every drop but that's not because I like it, it's because I get paid for it.

The door opens and I realise that we're in some kind of car park or garage. Low-ceilinged roof, concrete slab construction, strip lights that flicker. Mummy is beside me, waiting for me to get out. She looks angelic, face fixed up again, jacket and top done up again primly. Her eyes, those lovely eyes, look at me and smile.

'When do I get paid?' I ask, edging out of the car.

She smiles. 'That's the wrong question, darling,' she tells me. I feel the attraction again, she is so beautiful, so loving and tender. It's only the bastard organ between her thighs that I hate. It's only that useless male appendage, those inches of flesh that could so easily be incised and burned.

I step out of the car, out into the cold air that makes me shiver. 'What is the right question,' I ask innocently, voice hovering circa thirteen years old. I want to look around but can't, my eyes

---

are fixed on her.

'I'm the one who delivers,' she explains, sliding along the seat towards me. 'I'm the one who gets paid.'

'I don't understand,' I tell her. That's fucking obvious but there's nothing like stating it.

'I hope you don't hate me too much,' she says, almost apologetically. The door slams shut and the car accelerates away, leaving me shivering in the darkness. In a moment the tail lights have disappeared and the car might well have never existed.

Fuck! Stupid bitch! What the hell was I doing getting out of the car without the cash? I scream and my anger echoes away from me, like rolling thunder across the sky.

I am alone and lost. Did it really happen? My knickers are wet, my nipples are sore and my mouth still tastes of spunk. A deserted car park, a brutalist construction that tells me nothing. Zero information, the building tells me nothing I don't already know. I could be anywhere. The place is silent and empty. Row upon row of empty spaces, forlornly marked out in yellow paint and obscured by black tyre marks and the menstrual spillage from cars too wrecked to survive. In the futile light that's cast down by third generation strip lights there is nothing to see. No signs. No exits. No lifts.

I ache but I'm too tired for sustained anger. There's nobody to blame but me, a stupid bitch who gets all she deserves. I begin to walk despondently, dragging my heels as I head in the same direction as the car. No stamping down my heels because it gives me a kick, all I want to do is get out and get back to that stinking hovel I use to bed down during the day.

It's easy not to think. Just watch someone in emotional shock, some poor bastard who's lost a child or a lover. You can see it:

face collapsed, bodies shrivelled up, soul destroyed. Everything behind the eyes is dead, blanked off, the seething beasts within pushed back. All it takes is pain. All it takes is hurt.

That's how I am. Foetal. That's how I've been for so long. I don't want to think. That's why I fuck so much. So easy to do. And the body rules the mind, don't think otherwise. When I fuck I don't have to think. When I fuck I fuck, and if I hate the bastards I fuck then so much the better.

I walk across that tundral expanse of cold empty space, following the route that I imagine the black car has taken. The walls are scarred with graffiti, angular swathes of lurid colour which might be scripts from another civilisation for all I can make out.

The exit sign has been painted over and so I nearly walk past it, but up close a dull light can just be made out under the layers of indecipherable spray. I push the double doors and am greeted by the ammoniac stench of stale piss. The elevator is working, a dull groan of gears echoing around me when I press the button on the wall. This is the best thing that's happened to me all day. Stupid bitch, reduced to feeling grateful that a lift is working in some piss drenched car park in the middle of shitsville. I want to laugh and scream at the same fucking time.

After the piss puddles on the outside the inside of the lift is clean and dry. I should've guessed there and then. I get in and press the button for street level. The doors slide shut, creaking metal complaining as the mechanism jars into arthritic motion. Down. I lean back against the aluminium panel, eyes closed, limbs aching. How far from home?

Where is Terry? How far from home is he? My brother, two years older and fuck only knows where he is. Dead. Probably. But I don't want to think about that either. Terry belongs to another time and place and I don't even know why I'm thinking about this shit.

Bitch! How could I let myself be ripped off by that freak in a car?

See. Easy not to think. Easy not to feel. Close it all off, otherwise the energy's sucked out of you. Easier to suck on rancid cock than on useless emotion.

Down. The lift is moving, descending noisily. Down the shaft. Cheap Freudian image, the elevator sliding down the shaft, carrying a cheap slut too stupid to think about anything. Stupid bitch. Everything I get I deserve.

I look up suddenly, wondering how many storeys are left to go, trying to work out how far up I've been. How many layers of fetid air sandwiched in dull grey concrete? Air reeking of stale piss, calcified dog shit and carbon monoxide. No sign of how many levels, no indicator flashing numbers as the lift drops lower and lower. No sign of stopping either, the mechanical strain of steel in concrete is all I hear.

The sound echoes up the concrete shaft when I bang my fist against the door. I can hear the sound carry, contained by the angled cubic walls of concrete, like a blood line through the building. The lift is taking too long and I'm starting to get worried. My voice fills the empty space, merging with the banging of my fist and the knocking of the lift against the walls of the shaft. Too long. No car park can be this high. The spunk in the pit of my belly is turning over, as though it's going to explode inside me, bursting through the walls of my stomach to shower the dull aluminium panels with blood and jism.

Knocked off balance by the sudden stop. Door slides open before I regain my senses. Heart pounding like it wants to break free of the rest of my freezing torso. Door slides open and Mr and Mrs Normal are standing there, nuclear couple staring at me with wide eyed surprise.

'Where the fuck am I?' I demand, gritting my teeth real mean. I hate this place, where ever it fucking is, and I hate these sad eyed empty people. Vacuum people, never felt anything, never suffered, never lived.

'There's no need to swear,' she says, disapproving little bitch that she is.

He's eyeing my legs, white limbs emerging from shiny black leather. He likes that, they all do, every single one of them. That's how they see me, white body wrapped in leather, clothed in the shiny skin of dead animals. Dead animals again, clothed and perfumed from carcasses. That's me as well, another fucking carcass for them to screw.

I step forward and she screams. Frightens the shit out of me. In slow motion, freeze framing, image by image. She's screaming, lips drawn back and a picture of hate in her eyes. He's rushing forward, making a grab at me, crowding me back against the elevator wall. Her voice is drowning everything else out, nullifying my own shock, frightening me with her cold intensity. His arms on my shoulders, pushing me back, forcing me back. My head cracks against the wall, a dull thud that echoes inside and outside, blinded by pain. She's leaping forward. At last I react, dazed, I lash out, feel my fingers sink deep into her flesh. Another scream, another scream and I don't know if it's her or me. Blood on my fingers, blood pouring like dribbles of come from her eye.

Pain, buzzing like current through my head. I'm struggling, kicking with heels designed to hurt, clawing for flesh with arms pinned down at my side. She's screaming pure emotion at me, and her face is beautiful as the blood pours over her deathly pale skin. Those eyes are empty and I love her for it. The welcoming solvent smell, something over my mouth and nose and then the world collapses as I do.

♦

I stifle the urge to scream as I emerge reluctantly from the darkness. Like a face breaking water, I open my eyes and the world is fully formed around me. How much better the darkness, that place where nothing matters and I matter less than that. But here, now, I'm awake and silent, staring at the slim, uniformed nurse standing at the foot of the bed I'm lying in.

She's looking at a set of notes, a red clip-board in hand while she flicks idly back through the pages. Her uniform is prim and proper, shades of blue and white, watch hanging from her chest, white cap neatly in place. She's young but sexless, her hair pinned back under the cap, the starched uniform makes her body into something functional so she safely can look after the dysfunctional. A wide mouth and eyes that are magnified by round glasses, I watch her for a moment until the strength of my gaze impinges on her consciousness.

'Oh, you're awake,' she says, smiling broadly. She's waiting for me to respond, to smile back perhaps or to let out a squeal of surprise. 'How are you feeling?' she asks when I stare back without breaking silence.

'Where are my clothes?' I ask, realising that I'm wearing a shapeless hospital gown, a kind of straitjacket without the interesting arm attachments. Apart from this slip of cotton I'm naked, and I hate that. I hate being naked, I'm always dressed when I fuck, to be undressed is so natural it's sick.

'Don't worry about that,' she laughs chidingly, 'your clothes are the last thing you should be worried about.'

She's got watery blue eyes and they're looking at me with a mixture of annoyance and incomprehension. She's pissed off because I'm not concerned about me or what's happened to me, all I care about is my leather jacket and skirt. Stupid bitch can't figure out a person who doesn't wake up in hospital shit scared. I'm not talking, I don't want to give her the pleasure, there's a buzz in being awkward, it's one of the few pleasures I allow myself.

'The doctor asked to be called as soon as you regained consciousness,' she tells me, walking round to the side of my bed to press a red button on the wall.

It's a small room, there's another bed next to mine but it's unoccupied. There's a bed side cabinet with a jug of water becoming stagnant, a visitor's chair that'll never be used while I'm here, a few bits of medical equipment on the wall and beside the bed. By the side of the door, the only door into the room, is a porcelain wash basin with a single tap high on the wall. Despite the antiseptic smell, tinged with the accumulated biological odours of human bodies, the place looks dirty and run down.

She is looking at me again, standing at the end of the bed, big sad eyes trapped behind glass and yet looking at me as though I'm something nasty that's dropped from an orifice somewhere. Now she's as silent as I am, pissed off with me because I'm not acting the way a patient should act. I don't give a shit. I turn and look down at the cabinet beside the bed, wondering if my clothes have been stashed in there or not. Or perhaps they've taken my stuff to be fumigated or destroyed. I want my jacket back. I've eaten, puked, fucked, shit wearing that jacket, it's as part of me as the hair on my cunt.

'Where's my jacket?' I demand as soon as the doctor arrives. He's a balding, sickly looking bloke, weak eyes and no chin. A genetic reject, the sort that pays to have his flaccid cock sucked by unsafe, unhygienic, time bombed street whores like me.

'Your jacket, woman? The last thing you should be worried about is your jacket,' he scolds me, in that pompous prick way they teach them at Medical School. Thin wrists and bony fingers, I can see that he's going to be a piece of shit to step on. Have I sucked his poor excuse for a cock before? They all look the same to me, the bastards that pay for my mouth or cunt.

'Where's my fucking jacket?' I hiss, injecting venom into my voice. But it's so hard to be threatening when you're wearing a slip of cotton that has to be tied at the back like a baby's bib. I feel like laughing but I can see that Nursey's well pissed off with me and that disapproving look is just what I need.

'In case it has escaped you attention, young lady,' he informs me coldly, 'you have been subject to a serious assault. You were found unconscious in the street, and we have reason to believe you were sexually assaulted. You were sick on admission and there were traces of semen in your vomit. We could take no chances and had your stomach pumped, and again there were traces of semen in the contents of your stomach. Luckily there seem to be no serious injuries, you were drugged though, which will explain why you only have minor cuts and bruises.'

I stare at him. I'd swear he's got a hard on under that sexless white coat. His eyes, watery and weak, pools of piss to see through, stare at me intently. He's searching my face for emotion, waiting to see my eyes cloud with tears or harden with outrage. Nursey too, emotional vultures waiting to feast on my reaction. There's a pause, a moment of tense silence while they wait for me to speak. The moment stretches, elongates, becomes unbearable to them.

'We have to continue with our examinations,' the Nurse says, snapping first. The bitch, she's given him the cue to carry on, freeing him from the burden of silence.

'We have to carry out an internal examination to determine if you were raped,' he says, stressing "rape" so that it sounds like the act itself. 'Or sodomised,' he adds, with the kind of gleeful spite you get with religious fanatics demanding the end of the world.

'How long do I have to stay here?' I ask irritably.

'The examination itself shouldn't be too long,' he replies, 'less than an hour. The analysis may take longer. And of course the police are keen to interview you.'

'And can I go after that?'

'That's not a medical decision,' he says. 'The police may decide they need to interview you further. Now, do you have any further questions?'

'Yes. Where's my jacket?'

He shakes his head. 'Some men,' he tells me, his eyes widening with excitement, 'will put their penis where I wouldn't put the tip of an umbrella.'

Nursey's smirking. She thinks that's real funny. 'If only you could get your prick as hard as the tip of an umbrella you'd be better qualified to talk about it,' I tell him, smiling like I'm a thirteen year old angel. I like the colour he turns, his face boiling over with rage, the words stuck down somewhere in his throat so he can't speak.

Door slams and I can hear it echo through the building, and I swear my laughter is chasing the fucker down the corridor.

'Why are you so horrible?' Nurse asks me, sounding hurt and vulnerable. For a minute I swear she's the one about to burst into tears.

'Why are you so nice?'

She shakes her head, she doesn't understand. 'You don't have to be like this,' she says, and I hear the sadness in that voice. 'We're here to help you, we're not bad people.'

'Then help me,' I snap, lying back, looking up at the wide expanse of peeling paint that is the ceiling. The bitch is trying to guilt trip me, like it's my fault that the world is shit and I care more about my jacket than I do about me.

'You're so pretty,' she tells me softly, sorrowfully. She's standing beside me, looking all concerned, as though her anger has evaporated. Her name tag says Margaret O'Farrell, though I don't catch any accent when she speaks. She touches me gently, letting her fingers rest on my arm for a moment. 'So pretty, so very pretty. Do you remember what happened to you?'

I flash back: dumped in the middle of nowhere, trapped in the lift, attacked by that faceless couple... My nostrils are suddenly full of that solvent delirium, I want it back, want to find that sweet oblivion where there's nothing but nothing.

'Did they hurt you, love?' she asks, perhaps mistaking my silence for something else. She wipes my brow, her soft warm fingers stroking my skin tenderly. Her voice is a whisper of compassion, it speaks of tenderness the way my voice never could.

'I'm alright,' I tell her, quietly. Eyes closed and the feel of her fingers is soothing on my brow.

'You heard the doctor,' she reminds me, 'we have to examine you. Does it hurt down below? Did they hurt you there?'

'I feel okay.' There's no memory after the blackout, if they fucked me or buggered me then there's no pain left now. But then there's no pain in the throat where I puked up or when they pumped my spunk filled stomach clean.

'I have to examine you,' she sighs apologetically, 'I'll be gentle, I promise.'

A shrug and I sink deeper into the bed, my head resting on a pillow, limbs flat against the cool starched sheets, arms at my sides. Cadaverous, I stare up at the ceiling again, reminded of dried come peeling on my skin. I hear her snapping latex gloves on, I can imagine her slipping them on over her fingers, pulling them tight so that her flesh sticks to the powdered inner surface. Her sensibly flat shoes make a shuffling sound on the stone floor as she moves across the room and wheels a steel trolley towards the bed.

'So pretty,' she coos, drawing up close to the bed again. I avoid her eyes, I'm sick of her already, sick of her trying to be nice to me, sick of her trying to guilt trip me, sick of her, sick of me.

Slowly she draws the sheets back, letting the cold air slide over my body. There's no way I'm moving, so I lay back and stare at the ceiling, ignoring her fussing. Is she nervous? She's going to stick her fingers into my cunt, to penetrate me with fingers clad in rubber, like pricks in condoms. Does it make the bitch nervous? Or horny?

'This won't hurt,' she promises, forcing my legs apart, lifting my immobile limbs and moving them into place. I feel a blast of cold air across my cunt, emphasising my nakedness under the pathetic infantile gown. I swear she's mentally humming a tune, lost in the wonders of her healing profession, handling me like I'm too brain dead to move for myself.

'This might be a little bit cold,' she warns me, keeping up a running commentary as she squirts clear jelly onto her rubberised fingers. She holds it up to me, a thick wave of clear jelly balanced on her finger tips. There's a sorry smile on her face, apologising because she's going to rape me with her sterile fingers.

Pan Panziarka

I can't help the intake of breath as she slaps the fluid between my thighs, the cold translucent slime rubbed into my sex. She's smearing it over my pussy lips and then carefully between them, lubricating my cunt the way a queer lubricates his arse. She's working good and proper, no delicacy, swift, precise movements to grease up my snatch.

'That wasn't too bad, was it?' she asks, evidently happy with the slippery, icy cunt she's got to play with. 'Now, I've just got to check for bruising,' she tells me, with that same pathetic smile that's meant to reassure me. I want to punch her in the mouth, to watch the blood spurt from that mouth that's too wide for her face.

She peers down between my legs, the glistening folds of my sex magnified by her glasses. I part my thighs further, opening my pussy for her, letting her see the prize that so many men pay for. I reach down and pull my cunt lips open, I want her to see, I want her to enjoy the show. Squeezing hard I feel the oil inside me dribbling out, that cold lubricant warmed by the heat of my sex. It's good, her face is red now, I can see she's embarrassed, but fascinated by the way I touch myself, by the shameless way I expose my cunt to her clinical gaze. This isn't in her script, she's supposed to steal this from me, to rob me of the pleasure of exhibition. Bitch, I won't give her that, I'd rather piss in her face then give her that.

'Bruises?' I taunt her, smiling. For a moment the shielded gaze is gone, and I see pure hatred in her eyes. Hatred. Isn't that good, isn't that the best we can fucking hope for?

'No bruises,' she reports, beads of sweat appearing on her brow.

'Sure? You want to have another look?'

'It doesn't have to be this way,' she tells me reproachfully, retreating. She's a martyr once more, sad eyes, sad voice, heaping the guilt in my direction as if I bloody care.

'Then how does it have to be?' I demand, laughing. 'Tell me, Sister Motherfucking Theresa, saint and martyr. Tell me how it should be?'

She's tempted but thinks better of it. Instead she turns back to her trolley, a construction of steel tubes laden with the metallic instruments of bodily inspection. They look like implements of torture, designed to control and humiliate, designed in that universe of sadistic domination that is called a medical laboratory. I envy the sick, twisted minds that can come up with such poetic instruments of suffering, the sleek steel tongs, forceps, clamps, scissors, scalpels...

'I need to take some swabs,' she informs me.

'Spunk samples?' I guess, pulling my knees up further, opening my pussy in preparation. Like a bitch I'm in heat, excited by her fear and disgust. My nipples are hardening, puckering from the cold and from my excitement.

She turns to me holding a speculum, her gloved hand clutching it tightly. I know what it's for, and my smile of recognition gives me away. Silently she begins work, using it to force open my pussy, the steel jaws like ice inside the inner membranes of my sex. She steps back to look, my cunt held open by the shiny steel instrument. The cold air seems to circulate between my thighs, accentuating that delicious feeling of exposure.

I know she's dying to talk, but now she's frightened of me. Frightened of this wicked tongue and the obvious pleasure I'm getting from flaunting myself. There's no shame in me, if I can fuck in the street for cash then I can open my crotch for this saintly, martyred woman. The swabs go in, stroking the inside of my sex, going deep into my cunt, searching out the traces of spunk that I know aren't there. In and out, slowly she's fucking

---

me with swabs of cotton, her fingers flicking gently the sides of my pussy lips.

When I sigh I can feel her shudder. She's sickened by my pleasure and that makes it all the sweeter. My own fingers sneak down, searching for my clit, which aches to be stroked in time with her nervous, medical explorations. I like the idea of coming, of wetting those swabs with my secretions, letting the technicians in the lab know what a sick little whore I am.

'Stop that!' she snaps finally, out of patience with this patient.

I laugh and settle back, pressing my fingers into the slick, oiled groove of my sex. It feels good and I like it. Roughly she removes the speculum, slapping my hand away with her rubbery fingers as I try to keep it in. I make a note to steal it later, to grab it and the rest of her collection of tools.

'Please turn over now,' she orders, hardly able to contain her anger.

'What next?'

'I need to check your back passage,' she tells me. 'In case you were anally raped.'

'I'd know if that happened,' I tell her, but turn over onto my belly anyway. All of a sudden I'm a co-operative little creature, eager to help Nursey in her ministrations. The cool touch of the jelly squirted between my arse cheeks makes me smile, I can feel it sliding down nicely.

'Please sit up, lift one knee towards your stomach,' she directs me. And I do as I'm told, lifting my backside high in the air, offering her a view of my nicely rounded rear. I even part my buttocks for her, obligingly letting her look at the tight button she wants to feel under her fingers. The oozing jelly slides down between my arse crack and into my sex, which is still puffy and sensitive. Fuck it, I feel just so turned on by it all.

'Bruising?' I ask, twisting round to look over my shoulder at her. Red faced again, she can hardly tear her eyes away from my arsehole. 'Can you see anything?' I ask, sweet thirteen year old once more.

'No signs of damage,' she whispers softly.

I cock a finger and trace it from my cunt lips to my arsehole, a tantalisingly slow journey under my thighs. I let my finger stop at my arsehole, letting it rest for a moment, resting in the pool of lubricating jelly. It feels good as I press my finger in, through the slight resistance of my anal ring and into the tight warmth of my anal passage. Deep, I press my finger slowly into my arsehole, pushing it in as far as it would go. My arsehole clutches tightly at the intruding digit, holding on to it in a gesture of welcome.

'Please, don't do that,' she says, weakly, lips trembling.

'Preventive medicine,' I tell her, pushing my finger in and out slowly. Fucking myself in the arse with my fingers, aided by the antiseptic, sterile, oily, jelly she squirted for me.

'I have to cleanse you,' she says, suddenly snapping out of her daze. Before I've had a chance to respond she's marching across the room, briskly walking away from the display she's been enjoying so much.

I turn and watch her march back, no longer interested in anally masturbating myself. She's wheeling a stand across to me, a tall steel tube dangling a black bag connected to a length of hose. It looks like a blood line or a drip, some intravenous concoction fit to pierce my skin and pump straight into my veins. I try to read her expression, trying to make sense of what's going on in her closed little mind. Have I gone too far? Have I fucked her off so much that the bitch is going to get me back?

'What's this?' I ask, keeping the disquiet from my voice. I'm staring at her and then at the bag swinging lightly from the top of the stand and then at her again.

'Don't worry,' she tells me reassuringly, allowing a smile to unsettle across her face. 'This won't hurt, I promise. Now, on all fours again, please.'

She's using that medical tone of voice again, ordering me about as though I'm a brain impaired moron. I hesitate, suddenly afraid of what she's going to do to me. 'What if I refuse?' I ask, knowing that in asking I'm telling her that I won't refuse, but a battered sense of pride requires that I make a gesture, no matter how futile or worthless.

'That would be silly,' she tells me with a condescending smile. 'This is for your own good. We have to do this just to make sure that you haven't been assaulted.'

'But you know I haven't, you've checked, you've seen... I'd know if someone had butt fucked me, I'd know if some bastard had shot a prick load of come up my arse...'

Again I can tell that she's shocked, but this time she brushes that feeling away. She's going to get her own way, she's taking control this time. 'Do I have to call for the orderlies?' she asks. 'Do we really have to restrain you?'

'You'd like that, wouldn't you?' I sneer. Meekly I turn over, on hands and knees, backside exposed and up in the air. On hands and knees again, it's a familiar position, my natural station in life. Hands and knees, body exposed and vulnerable, that's how they like me.

She parks the stand by the side of the bed, the long steel tube clanging against the bed frame and striking a pleasantly discordant note. There's nothing on the bag, no sign of what it contains but I can see by the way it ripples and sags that it contains liquid of some kind. It's pierced at the bottom by a long rubber tube that hangs limply, pulled down by the weight of a small bulb at the end and a valve to control the flow.

My arsehole is still lubricated, wet and slippery after the way I'd arse frigged myself. Only now it feels open, exposed, like a cunt but worse. She squirts some more jelly on her fingers, eyes intent as she applies it to my anal rim, her fingers tracing the sensitive rear lips without pressing into me. I'm certain she's enjoying herself, the bitch knows that I'm easy meat now. My carcass is hers, hers because she's medical and I'm the subject. Subject. Object. Victim with no voice because whatever she does is good for me.

'This might be a little uncomfortable,' she warns, quoting from the first page of the book of medical lies.

I close my eyes as I feel the nozzle penetrating from the back, pushed against the wet resistance of my arsehole and then deeper into my rectum. It pierces and takes possession, a length of rubber tubing like a miniature cock slipping up my lubed arse. She's working silently, pushing that tube with rubber gloved fingers, eyes sparkling with an excitement that she would never admit to. Poor martyred bitch, she's doing this because she's a saint and I'm a sinner, she's healthy and I'm sickness itself.

'How's that?' she asks, not even pausing. The tube goes higher, rubbing against the sensitive flesh inside my arsehole. I don't reply, there's no funny answer waiting to spring from my lips and grab her by the throat.

'This won't hurt,' she repeats. I tense, expecting the worst as she begins to pump the small rubber bulb at the end of the tube. She could be spraying herself with scent the way she squeezes that bulb, pumping it gently. It feels like there's a balloon expanding inside me, filling up with short bursts of air. It widens, pushing against the ring of anal muscle until it's snug, a tight fitting rubber plug that means I can't pull the tube out without hurting myself.

Next she loosens the valve and the flow of warm liquid starts to trickle into my rectum. It pours through the tube and into my body, soaking my guts with its smoothly regulated flow.

'An enema,' I whisper as my guts begin to fill up.

'Just try to relax,' she suggests, smiling sadly. 'You're so pretty, I can see why you were attacked,' she adds.

The enema is trickling slowly, I can feel every drop as it fills and suffuses, taking occupation inside me. It feels so strange, already I'm sure that my stomach's starting to bulge. It's not a bad feeling, only there's nothing I can do to control it.

'Such lovely long legs,' she says, and I'm not sure if she's talking to me or to herself. She touches me, stroking my legs softly, running her fingers up and down the pale skin of my thighs. Her rubber fingers feel warm against my skin, the latex glove warmed by the heat of her body. Up and down slowly, more firmly, along the inside of my thigh. 'You are so pretty,' she repeats wistfully, becoming more insistent.

'Enjoying this?' I ask weakly, closing my eyes because I'm beginning to enjoy it. Shit, I don't want to feel pleasure, I want to feel outrage instead, but the feel of her fingers stroking my inner thigh resonates with the strange feelings being pumped through my backside.

'So pretty yet so nasty,' she whispers. Her fingers go up and down, only now they linger at the top of my thighs, at the opening of my cunt which is becoming wet. Her fingers stroke my pussy lips, almost accidentally at first but then again and again. She is lost, her eyes glaze over as she handles me the way she wants. I don't resist, I don't say or do anything. When her fingers press against my swelling clit I sigh and move back, wanting to feel her fingers inside my cunt. My backside is rounded, offered up temptingly so that she can finger my pussy while the water surges through my rectal passage.

'Oh...' I whisper, surprised by the wave of pleasure that passes through me when her fingers slip into the wetness of my sex. It feels good and I want more of it. I can't believe what a stupid bitch I am for feeling so fucking hot, but she's turning me on. This bitch is no one's fantasy nurse, there's no rubber uniform, no high heels, no bursting cleavage or fetish fashion, but she's got me so horny I can't say no.

I sigh, moan, push my backside higher in the air, open myself, moan and sigh some more. I can't control it. Her fingers are fucking me, slipping in and out, slurping obscenely with the wetness of my desire. My cunt bud throbs and swells as she strokes it, making my eyes roll with pleasure.

'Oh... No...,' I sigh, arching my back as I climax powerfully, my whole being resonating with that blast of pleasure from the core of my sex. I feel weak but I'm still on hands and knees and my pumped up stomach feels fit to burst.

'So pretty, even when you come,' she informs me with a smile. She brings her fingers to my face, shows me the moisture she's milked from my pussy. I smell cunt and latex, the translucent rubber gloves laced with my cunt juices, glistening seductively. I know what she wants, I lick my come from her fingers, suck up the essence of my orgasm and let it linger in my mouth.

'Have you finished, Nurse?'

We both turn and that single moment of complicity is broken by the presence of the doctor. Our roles are fixed and we return to them, seeking the comfort and security they offer. Nurse and patient, an angel of mercy and a pathetic creature with her naked arse in the air. My face colours, stupid bitch that I am I have allowed my weakness to get the better of me. I had granted her power and she used it to fuck me with fingers I couldn't even feel, fingers wrapped in the anti-septic safety of latex gloves.

'I think this is nearly empty,' she says, moving quickly to check the enema bag. She squeezes it, forcing the last few drops of liquid into my rectum. I'm full, a pregnant belly bulging obscenely. Now I feel the discomfort, like I'm fit to explode shit and piss across the room. There's no control left to me, I don't even control my shit function any more. And, even worse, I'm still incredibly turned on by it. Bitch! I hate myself, I loathe myself for being so pissing weak that I can't resist.

'Empty her now,' the doctor orders, in much the same way he'd tell her to empty the garbage.

'No... I want to do this in private,' I protest. They can't expect me to do in front of them, they just can't. No, I can't, I can't. A voice is screaming inside my head, I don't want to do it. I want to shit in private, it's my right, my privilege to shit the stuff out away from their greedy eyes.

'No,' he tells me, eyes smiling behind an emotionless mask. 'It has to be done here, now.'

He knows. She knows it too. It's a power trip. *They control when I shit.* Jesus, they even control what I'm going to shit. The bastards, they've filled my guts so that I can empty myself in front of them. I'm going to explode and I can't stop myself. I feel sick. Hatred and anger surge through me and smash against the rocks of helplessness. I can't move, the tube is lodged inside me, forcing my buttocks apart, pressure on my tight little arsehole.

Nurse doesn't need to be told twice. Smirking, she crosses the room to get a cardboard bowl, a grey, papery shit bowl for me to use. I feel sick but there's nothing to bring up, they've already washed the contents of my stomach out. Now they're going to wash the contents of my bowels out too. My nipples are hard and they rub against the cotton slip, my cunt is still wet and I'm sick with myself.

The valve is closed off and somehow a portion of the rubber hose is removed. I can move more freely but I've still got something wedged inside me. 'Single Bardex?' the doctor asks, professionally keen to ensure procedure is being followed.

'I didn't have a double Bardex valve available,' she explains earnestly, speaking their language so that I'm just some dumb bitch who doesn't need to know. I'm not there for my brains, I'm there because they need my body. The grey bowl is placed between my legs and I'm hauled up onto my knees.

'Remove the robe,' the doctors decides, 'we don't want to get it dirty.'

I'm naked, my skin puckering gooseflesh as the cool air strokes me. Nipples like cherries, long pale legs parted obscenely, a weeping of desire trailing from my sex. And the plug in my behind, poking out like a little plastic turd. Sick. Sick!

Nurse is messing around, playing with the plug, moving it from side to side and making me shiver. It feels good. It feels sick and disgusting. The doctor's watching approvingly, a knowing expression on his face as he studies my nakedness. I swear he's got a hard on under that white coat, under the body armour of the pure at heart.

I scream, tears pouring down my face, tracking unfamiliar

Pan Panziarka

territory, virgin soil unused to tears. The shit explodes from my arse, an obscene projectile sludge that splats into the grey bowl. It takes forever, a slurry that pours and pours until I'm empty. Really empty. Nothing left inside me. No crap in my bowels and no pride in my soul.

'Good. Send that for analysis,' doctor says. 'There may be semen samples we can use,' he adds.

'Yes, doctor,' comes the reply, meek and mild in the presence of his highness. She wipes me quickly, using a wet, disinfected wipe, as though I'm a child who's just shit herself. She wipes carefully, cleans it all away, caresses my tender arsehole so that the pleasure lurking there is brought to the surface. Pleasure? I feel sick with myself. Evil bitch, how could I? How could I?

Doctor steps forward. 'This will help you sleep,' he tells me coldly. It stings and I cry out again as he forces something up my arse. For one sick moment I'm sure it's his cock, rigid with excitement after witnessing my humiliation. He removes his gloved fingers and the drug begins to work, absorbed into the blood stream from within my rectum.

'I want my jacket...' I whimper as the blackness comes rushing back to me.

THREE

Eyes closed but awake, drifting aimlessly because my body won't uncurl from its foetal warmth. Wrapped safe in layers of cotton, I hardly dare to move, I just want to laze and relax. At the back of my mind there's a nagging thought that something's wrong, but I don't want to follow it. No idea what time it is, or whether I've slept for hours, days or minutes. I drift in and out of sleep, hesitating on the blurred border between the two, knowing that so long as I don't move I can stay here where nothing hurts and nothing means anything.

Is it morning? I listen carefully and as I do so I'm pulled away from sleep completely. There is something wrong. There's silence. There's never silence in hospital, not even in the dead of night when they take the dead away. The Nazi hierarchy of hospital organisation, the class structure of ancillaries, cleaners, porters, clerks, caterers, bureaucrats, a dozen varieties of nurse, a dozen breed of doctors and their hangers on, they can't be silent, it's against the law. The corridors should be echoing to trolleys, beds, wheel chairs, the muttered oaths of the underpaid and over worked, the booming voices of the hospital aristocracy...

I open my eyes when the door opens and I watch Nursey creep in, flat shoes almost silent, only the faint swish of her starched uniform giving her away. She walks directly to the foot of the

---

bed and looks at the notes, scribbles something down and only then does she look at me.

'Did you sleep well?' she asks brightly.

Has she forgotten? Has this stupid bitch forgotten? She forced an enema up my arsehole, filled me to bursting then let it explode from my body so that her doctor could get his rocks off. Did that mean nothing to her? Shit. This bitch could make a million providing professional humiliation services out on the streets. A cold hearted slut like her could clean up by cleaning up, scooping those enema freaks for every penny they've got.

'What time is it?' I ask her sullenly.

'It's morning,' she smiles brightly. 'Now, just the daily jobs first. Temperature and blood pressure first.'

'Gonna take them up my arse as well, are you?' I sneer, feeling really vicious. I can't forgive the bitch, I can't. I remember that I don't know where my poxy jacket is, and that pisses me off even more.

'Don't be like that,' she tells me, sadly. I swear it's like nothing ever happened. Shit, maybe I imagined it. Perhaps I fantasised that she frigged me, or that I fingered my arsehole for her, or that she filled my guts with water so that they could be publicly emptied later on.

She gives the thermometer a shake and then sticks it under my tongue before I can say any more. I let her take my pulse, I've got no fucking use for it. Then the strap around my arm so she can take my blood pressure. All the time I'm wondering how long I've been out cold. What are the chances of the same nurse being on duty all this time? Something's not right, why can't I hear the rest of the hospital?

'Good,' she announces, evidently satisfied that I've got a pulse, a temperature and a blood pressure. 'I shouldn't really be telling you this,' she whispers conspiratorially, 'but we've not been able to find any evidence of a sexual assault.'

'Does that mean I can go?' I ask, hopefully. There's a whole lot more I want to say, but I bite my tongue because all I want to do is get out.

'Yes, I should think so,' she tells me, happily. 'Only the doctor wants to see you first, but I should think you'll be out of here soon.'

'What the fuck does he want?'

She glares at me, her face narrowing disapprovingly, her temporary faith in me smashed again. 'I do not understand why you are so hostile all the time,' she says, pronouncing every syllable just so that I know she's angry.

'I'm not the one who's hostile. Shoving a rubber tube up someone's arse is a pretty hostile sort of act if you ask me,' I reply, enjoying the confusion on her face.

'I just think you're a bad person,' she says quietly, delivering the words with a quiet solemnity that's entirely fitting. She's done her level best, poor martyred creature, goodness embodied in her starched bosom, and yet she's been rejected and abused by my wicked mouth at every turn. Poor cow, how my cunt bleeds for her. Still, she's reached a conclusion, I'm a bad person, so taking control of my shit function was no bad thing. It's what I deserve.

The door swings open and her partner in anti-crime is there, clothed in the white character armour of his profession. Once he would have worn a bloodied butcher's apron, stained and stenched in blood and gore. Now he's clothed in the white purity of science instead of the bloodied red of superstition. The stethoscope around his neck like an amulet to ward off evil, a towering colossus of a man who's pissed, shit and puked his way through medical school. A doctor, God's chosen representative now that the church is fucked, I'm supposed to feel humbled by his proximity. The moment I set eyes on him I want to lash out, I'd wrap that fucking stethoscope around his balls and rip his testicles across the room. As a doctor he can humiliate and abuse in the name of medical science, he can cause pain and suffering in the name of humanity. Auschwitz is his testament to medical science, his monument to humanity and to healing, we're all *untermensch*.

I swear he's got a hard on again. I know these things, I get paid to turn soft, lifeless bits of flesh that little bit harder, that's my blood sport, transferring it from brain to cock the way only a whore can. There's a scale of rigidity that's reflected in the eyes, and every time I stare into those lifeless pools of piss I know his cock's just too stiff for him to touch. Maybe that's why he hates me. They do that – can't get it hard with anyone but a cheap whore and so they blame the whore. That's why they hate us. That's why so many of us wind up cut to pieces in the middle of shitsville. And this nasty looking specimen, who belongs in a jar with his organs hanging limply by his face, looks like the type who'd make a career of cutting cheap whores into bin sized chunks of flesh for him to wank over.

'The results have come back from analysis,' he announces, as though he's telling a theatre full of people and not just me and Nurse in this pissy little room. 'We can find no evidence of semen from the vaginal swabs or from the rectal matter that was collected yesterday.'

'So you mean,' I ask him earnestly, 'that when I said I'd know if I'd had a cock up my arse I was right?'

He can't help it. The man has no control, his face brightens and the sweat masses at the top of the hair line. He's fighting to control his cock and he can't do that and think at the same time. 'Young lady,' he splutters, and I know he's on the edge of orgasm, 'you lead a singularly disgusting lifestyle. It behoves me to warn you to stop, to change your way of living. It's dangerous, physically as well as morally...'

'Are you telling me you want a freebie? What do you want, doc? A quick blow job? Or how about a quick game of concentration camp doctor?'

I love the look on his face. 'You disgust me,' he hisses, only he's telling me he loves me.

Nurse is upset, she can't handle this at all. She slaps me hard, the back of her hand swiped across my face. Brightness around the eyes, a quick electric burst of pain and then I'm left with the taste of blood in the mouth. I touch my lips and stare at the blood, so rich and colourful I'd spray the walls with it.

'Hold her down!'

Nurse obeys, she launches herself across me and pins my shoulders down. I'm not struggling, I let her hold me down, half hoping that I can spit my blood into her pretty little mouth.

'Do you know what it's like, pandering to people like you?' he demands, body shaking with emotion. 'Day in, day out I come face to face with the dregs of a society that's too weak to clean itself up. In better days you would have died from filth and disease, you and your kind would have been left to rot. Now we've lost our Darwinian instincts. We suffer you to live and allow you to destroy the rest of society by your sick example. Human effluent, no pride or dignity left inside you, I would sacrifice you for the good of humanity.'

'You sick bastard,' I mutter, unresisting, pressed down by Nursey who's surprisingly strong. I feel strangely relieved, like it's good that this is happening. It feels right, to strip away the mask of science to see the true fascist face of medicine in all its frenzied glory. He's revelling in it, the delight in his eyes, the face of a Fuehrer gazing down at the adoring masses who worship the hard cock they secretly desire.

He begins to unbutton the white coat, trembling hands struggling with thick round buttons. 'You don't deserve treatment, you don't even deserve our pity. No better than animals...'

I watch in silence as he struggles out of his clothes, trousers undone at the top, underwear pulled down, white coat hanging loose, hard prick grasped lovingly in his fist. And he is hard, the way I knew he would be. That gleam in his eye, that fascist glory look is pure sex. It's what I deserve, bitch that I am, it's all my fault. He's nearly there, a few more insults, a few more threats, some more verbal humiliation and then he stumbles forward, yanking down hard on his precious organ. White spray arcs over my face and neck, splashing wetly onto my chin and into my waiting mouth. Isn't this what he's been waiting for? To shoot his load into the hungry mouth of a shiftless, worthless, piece of human shit.

I lick my lips, chasing every last drop of his come into my mouth. I let it linger there, on my tongue, a pool of warm, salty juice from his cock. My medicine, this is what I'm here for, doctor. This is good for me. This is what every whore wants: her doctor's spunk in her mouth.

I spit it out, spewing it out like venom straight into Nursey's mouth. 'See!' I laugh, fucking hysterical, 'I'm a martyr too. I'm a Christian, I care about the good of mankind too, fuckers! That's what you've been waiting for, isn't it, bitch? You've got it now, his slimy spunk straight into your mouth. If that isn't a work of charity I don't know what the fuck is.'

'Sedate her,' is what the doctor orders, hurriedly getting dressed again.

Nurse swallows a mouth full of spit and spunk. She wants to force my mouth open and tongue it clean properly, to suck every last drop of fluid that her esteemed medical colleague has seen fit to deposit inside me. It's a nightmare but a safe one. Who's going to believe a whore like me? They've got the power here, I am theirs because I'm a worthless patient and they're latter day saints.

'Aren't you going to clean my arsehole first?' I scream as my robe is ripped open. 'Aren't you going to piss on me as well?' as Nurse positions my breast. 'Or do you want to take turns in buggering me?' as the needle is plunged into my nipple.

I scream. Sweat pours from my face, lips drawn back, my whole being concentrated in one small nub of flesh held tight between finger and thumb. Blood red nipple leaking blood where the needle has scored the soft flesh. I scream but there's no fight in me. Held down. The pain pulsing rhythmically where the steel tipped needle has entered my flesh.

'You should never have been born,' Nurse whispers, her hot breath close against my breasts. 'You people should be sterilised at birth, bred out of the race to improve the strain...'

I'm sinking as the pain grows, not in my flesh but in my head. Towering, growing, overwhelming everything else. The needle is expunged and then stabbed down again, cutting into the million nerve endings in my nipple. This is where I should feel pleasure. This is where nature intended I suckle my young. Again. Needle sinking into bloodied flesh, lightning strike of intense white pain.

Sinking. Lower, lower. Darkness swallowing me up as I am left with nothing but the feeling of pain. I can't move, trapped in a background noise of pain and raw sensation, sizzling like current in the brain. I can see myself, lying helpless, eyes staring up at the ceiling and seeing nothing. The topography of my terror is stretched before me, peaking on breasts disgorging blood not milk from punctured nipples.

I can see myself. I am looking down, floating in this torture chamber above my prostrated self and the Auschwitz medical team at my side. She is staring at me, wide eyed, wild eyed, out of her senses with lust and pleasure. He is in control, body rigid with delight. I am the *Unterbitch*, the embodiment of human genetic sewage to do with as he wishes. In the interests of science. For the good of man.

'The patient is undergoing convulsions, sir,' Nurse reports breathlessly, toying with my bloodied nipples. I scream inwardly, the play of her fingertips on my flesh like fire in the brain. Voiceless, motionless, my immobile body makes no response.

He understands though, there's a wicked smile on his face, he can understand the torment of pure pain when the body is out cold. A technician of body sensation, each nuance of agony has its own special meaning, a semiotic of suffering that is unique. It's his mother tongue, the only language he is fully versed in. And me? Stupid fucking bitch, I'm about to learn it word for word.

Equipment is wheeled into the room, a square box on wheels which sports lights and wires in profusion. I watch from my strange vantage point, as Nurse carefully positions the box by the side of my limp body. Doctor is scrubbing up in the sink, attacking his hands with soap and water, disinfecting himself so that he can disinfect me. My mouth is open, I struggle through the pain, struggle to become real again, but my mouth can only leak a trail of cold spit. Like a limp dick, the more I try to force a reaction the less there is.

Why didn't I keep my sick mouth shut? Why did I have to scream and be difficult? This is what I deserve. It's my fault, it's always my fucking fault.

Nurse soothes my nipples, she rubs on some thick, creamy salve, the whiteness becoming pink with my blood. It feels like heaven. Bulging nipples fit to burst are rubbed even harder, pleasure and pain overlaid so that I can't tell where one ends and the other begins. She squirts more gunge onto my nipples, her smile broadening as she realises that my nips are becoming more erect. Bitch! I hate myself. Why is it? Why do I have to feel pleasure when there should be nothing but pain and disgust?

Thighs are forced apart, opened obscenely, pink cunt flesh on show. Nurse reaches down and starts rubbing her fingers in and out of my wet snatch. I shiver, screaming behind expressionless eyes, as the pleasure pierces me. I'm wet because I'm a whore with no control over her own body. In and out, Nurse is really giving it to me, her fingers squelching in the oozing, gaping hole down between my legs. She teases my clit then pinches down hard, I want to spasm but can't... How many fingers? My pussy is being forced open, cunt lips wide apart as she's using three, four, five fingers to fuck me with. She's taken possession, using her hand to invade my cunt, going in as hard and as deep as she can, a clinical invasion of vagina and womb.

A background radiation of pain, a gnawing, biting ache at the back of the head, is punctuated by her fisting of my cunt. It feels as though my whole body is cleaved open. This isn't sex, this is rape, this is war. Doctor is watching, cool clinician observing technique and ready to offer advice should his protégé falter. Spit bubbles from my mouth the way cunt juice bubbles around her fingers. It must be blood but I can't tell.

'Strap her down now,' doctor orders, satisfied that I have been knuckled enough.

'Yes, doctor,' comes the meek reply. She takes a second to wipe her fingers on my belly, the wet rubber cleansed on my clammy flesh. She's smiling. Fucking bitch enjoying every second of this particular medical procedure. I hate her. I scream inside, burning up with pain and anger. I'd fucking fist her arse so wide her entrails would wind up splattered all over the walls.

Leather straps are used to bind my upper arms, wrists, ankles and thighs to the sides of the bed. A hospital bed is a bondage dream come true, so many places to attach straps, a bed designed as an instrument of torture and nothing else. In seconds I am stretched out, tied down, strapped, bound, attached, a piece of the bed itself. My mouth is forced open and something inserted over my tongue. I can't breath, waves of silent panic pour through me. I want to die, Jesus, let me die...

Gagged tightly, my breath rises and falls quickly, forced through my nostrils. I'm scared. Please, let it end. I'm looking down at myself and yet every emotion is amplified because I can see what's happening. I don't want this to happen. I don't want this to happen. I don't...

The box of tricks by the bed is powered up, it wakes with a low, ominous hum of current. Doctor is flicking switches, turning dials, selecting that personal setting he's been saving for shit whores like me. Nurse stands on the other side of the bed, the sweat pouring from her face, tracking from under her cap. Her skin is flushed pink with excitement and I guess she's come half a dozen times.

'What setting?' she asks, her voice hesitant.

'Don't worry, she'll feel it,' he tells her. He turns to me and smiles. 'It's time to cleanse that filthy brain of yours,' he tells me. 'But don't worry,' he adds maliciously, 'this is going to hurt like hell.'

I can't even close my eyes, nor look away. I am forced to watch, sickened and afraid, as he proceeds with cool deliberation. He was born to medicine, it's his one true vocation, his natural place in the world just as mine is on my knees with a length of cock in my mouth. He flips open the top of his Pandora's box, red warning messages and SS skulls decorate the panel display. He carefully unravels the coiled probes, long, flexible lengths of cable tipped with copper clamps.

There's no need for him to say it. Nurse takes a probe, snaps the clamp open and runs her finger along vicious reptile teeth. These teeth were made to hurt, specially designed, super-serrated, high tensile nipple cutters. Tears pour from my expressionless eyes, eyes that are dead to everything. I cannot scream any louder, in my head the walls are shaking and the glass is shattering. First one nipple, big, round, erectly sensitive, is mashed and then the other. It feels as though they are operating, the needles into my nipples were clean compared to the filthy, raw edge of pain that spurts like blood in the brain.

Blindness. My body jolts, shaking the bed as the current flames through me. Pure current: white, incendiary, powerful. It blasts through my nipples, lava flows into my body. The straps hold me into place as my body shudders and pulls to break free. Animated by the electricity the good Doctor treats me with, I want death to end it all. I cannot turn away. I cannot stop it. I hover above my body and watch as the switch is thrown again and the electricity singes my nipples and makes my body go rigid.

Tears pour down my face. I'm screaming for it to stop. Begging, pleading like an animal but there's nothing but tears to tell anyone I'm even alive. Reduced to a disjointed lump, a thing of tissue, bone and mucus. Jesus fucked, let it end...

Nurse makes a sudden movement. She's on her knees, down there in front of the bed. She'll not be denied this time, her prize is there to be claimed. She unbuttons his white coat, freeing the only flesh she really worships. There's a pause as she begins to suck the Doctor's cock, feasting on it deliriously. And then the pain returns, in his excitement he throws the switch again and his pleasure is turned into my agony.

Wracked with sweat, body contorting endlessly as the current puts me through hell. My flesh is burning, nipples welded to metal. A white torrent of pain is burning into my skull, eroding, cutting, burning, slashing, destroying... Let it end, Jesus let it end.

Doctor's breathing harder and harder. He's close to orgasm, close to his own blinding white light of sensation. One long burst of power, one last session of pure hell. My cunt is leaking piss, pouring freely over my thighs and settling in a pool under my backside. My body is straining against the straps that hold me down, straps that cut into me as surely as the metal clamps on my breasts.

Finally reduced to a body, more dead than alive, a heaving, stinking thing of flesh basted in its own piss. Less than human. And in their concentration camp excitement Doctor and Nurse can hardly be happier. She's moving like a practised bitch, on all fours like a good little slut and working her mouth over his Nazi length of cock. His eyes are burning with a febrile, hysterical, body burning joy. Strength through joy, purity through pain.

Nurse swallows it all, taking great mouthfuls of holy come as her privilege. She has served her profession well, as well as he has served his. Inside my head there's nothing but defeat and suffering. The flow of current is over, but I understand with a finality that makes me want to puke, that the clamps are destined for my cunt next.

FOUR

What would life without suffering be? So sweet. A gift. Let me close my eyes to die for it. A life without suffering? There's always a first time. The universe hates us all, but malicious fucking beast that it is it leaves open a dream of a life without misery. Imagine that. A whole life, complete without pain, suffering or regret. What a dream, we'd all have that. Fuck intelligence or meaning, fuck it all. A life without suffering, sweet vision be mine, work backwards through my life. Unwork this pain and horror, undo the darkness. Make me whole, make me unhuman. Please.

'It's over now, you're safe,' a voice whispers. A voice so soft it barely impinges on my consciousness. This is a voice of goodness and trust, this is a voice that cannot lie or do harm. I must be dreaming.

When my eyes open I am bathed in light, filtered through a big square window that seems to tower above my bed. I close my eyes again, fighting the pull of the real, reaching back to the darkness which is my natural home. The light dances on my closed eye lids, orange visions that detract and distract.

'It is safe, I promise,' the voice tells me, as though reciting a poem.

Pan Panziarka

'Where am I?' I ask, and my voice is coarse and suspicious besides the pure voice that addresses me so sweetly.

'Somewhere safe. You'll be looked after here, there's no need to worry.'

Eyes open, catch sight of the pretty young woman beside me, and then close again. 'Am I still in hospital?'

'No, you're not in hospital now,' I'm told, though there's a note of hesitation in this sweet voice.

'How did I get here?'

A pause. 'You were brought here last night, from the hospital.' Another pause while she, whoever she might be, tries to work out what to tell me. 'You seem to have suffered some kind of spiritual breakdown...'

'A what?' I sit up in bed, bolt upright, staring straight at her, who stares back in alarm. What the fuck is this? Whores don't have spiritual problems, we have mental breakdowns, we have manias and frenzies that end in psychotic and self-destructive violence.

'A spiritual problem that led to some kind of seizure...' my new friend explains, her clear blue eyes meeting my own so that I can see the sincerity blazing forth. 'I'm not a medical expert,' she adds, in case I suspect her of dangerous medical tendencies.

'Who told you I suffered a seizure?' I ask, amazed at my own self-control.

'It's what the hospital reported to Sister Catherine.'

I nod. The Nazi bastards have packed me off to some kind of nut house run by religious freaks, the work of science completed

---

now it's time my soul is saved. That makes sense of course, anything I say now can be dismissed as the ravings of a lunatic whore, probably suffering some kind of syphilitic mental decay. What do I say? Where do I begin?

'You'll be well looked after here,' I'm informed with a smile that is totally genuine.

'Do you know who and what I am?' I ask, unable to resist the temptation any longer.

'It doesn't matter what you've done in the past,' she tells me earnestly, touching my arm. 'What matters is what's inside a person, nothing else.'

I laugh. It's the doctor's spunk inside me that's important, nothing else. I laugh and she merely smiles, her blue eyes staring at me seductively. 'It's good that you're laughing, we want you to be happy here.'

'Can I leave?' I ask suddenly. A jolt of fear makes me go weak at the knees as I imagine my leather jacket going to its death in the concentration camp incinerator at the hospital.

'Our Sister will explain all of that to you,' I'm told. 'I'll go and fetch her shortly. Normally we share a communal lunch, but as it's your first day would you like some bread and cheese and some fruit?'

I nod. No meat but it'll do, it feels like I haven't eaten for days. 'Yes, please.'

She smiles. 'You're going to like it here,' she affirms, 'I can tell.'

This time I'm taking no chances. It's a small room made bigger by the light that pours promiscuously through the window. The hospital robe has been mysteriously replaced, instead I'm

Pan Panziarka

clothed in a one piece night dress that looks fuck proof. I'm naked underneath, of course. What did Nursey do to me once I was under? I feel strangely blank, as though there should be more that I know. It hurts and I don't want to think, I don't want to push. All I can think is that she wanted to fuck me, conscious or unconscious, alive or dead. That bitch was going to screw me one way or another, and so I guess she did when she had the chance.

I look out of the window and am disappointed with the view. Green fields, trees on the horizon, a fleck of silver that might be a river or a lake. The bastards have dumped me in the middle of the country, miles from the polluted grey streets that are my natural home. I hate the countryside, full of slow witted cousin fuckers, frightened Nazis and animals that stink too much to eat raw. Shitsville was better, concrete and piss I can relate to, green fields and flowing rivers are a language I don't understand.

My heart skips a beat. Things must be looking up. There's a wardrobe on one side of the room, my jacket's hanging up, tattered and weather beaten but all my own. I slip it on, let it wrap its arms around me like a welcoming lover. What a pathetic, sentimental bitch I am, I almost feel like crying.

Back into bed, my feet are cold on the tiled floor. There's something inside my head, some barrier that I come up against when I try to think back to what happened in the hospital. Nothing. No clear memory, only a vague uneasy feeling. I have suffered I know that much, but how and why are mysteries. I don't want to think about it, so I don't. I sit on the bed, wrapped in leather, hands deep in pockets and wait.

'Why have you got your coat on?' my friend asks, returning with a tray loaded with hunks of bread, cheese and a couple of apples.

'I feel safer with this on,' I explain, digging my hands deeper into the pockets. My jacket stinks, stale cigarettes, sweat, semen, perfumed biologically by the very process of my existence. It smells of me, my cigarettes, my sweat, spunk I sucked for money. Like an aura, a halo, I am enveloped and protected by my stink.

She nods, she doesn't know what the fuck I'm talking about but she accepts it all the same. She is wearing a long dark dress, a shapeless piece of material that reaches down to her ankles. The bitch looks real good in it too, so sweet and angelic, she'd look good in sackcloth and ashes. Her eyes are so very blue, she'd make a fortune on the street, eyes like that can turn a man's cock to stone.

'I've brought you some food,' she tells me, bringing the tray towards me. She carefully places the tray on the edge of the bed, smiling charitably all the time.

'Thanks,' I say, returning a smile. I pick up the cheese and a knife, short, sharp and with a serrated edge. I trace my thumb gently across the edge of the knife, testing the sharp teeth with my skin. One swoop and I could slit her throat, the blood would spurt across the room and she'd topple over, clutching her wounded throat. She's watching me, her eyes drawn to the play of my finger on the knife, is she nervous?

'Sister will see you later this afternoon,' she tells me, deliberately looking away from the knife.

'What the fuck are you doing here?' I ask her, intrigued by her presence here. Someone so young and pretty should have a life to lead. Stuck here looking after losers is no life to lead, not for anyone.

She's shocked by my question. 'I'm looking after you,' she tells me. 'Hospitals tend to the physically sick, but who will fend for the spiritually ill? The work we do here is just as important, the body cannot be well as long as the sickness resides in the spirit.'

I cut into the cheese and laugh. 'Shit, girl, what the fuck's wrong with you? You could be out having some fun somewhere... You don't really believe all that religious shit, do you?'

She nods, smiling sadly. 'You have no faith,' she tells me quietly, 'but I do. There's so much evil in the world and yet the tiniest bit of faith will tear it all away. That's all there is to it, faith. Don't you think you could have faith?'

'I don't go for that sort of shit.'

'But look at the Bible,' she replies, the passion making her more animated. 'Why is it that so many of the prophecies have come true?'

'I don't believe any of that shit,' I tell her, beginning to enjoy the argument.

'But how can you say that...'

'Because it's shit, all of it. Religion is a fucking con game,' I explain between mouthfuls of bread and cheese. 'It's there to keep us all in our places. The reward's in the next life so we suffer like fuck in this one.'

She won't accept that, poor deluded bitch. Her eyes are filling with tears of conviction, certain in her faith that she is right and I am wrong. 'You just need to open your heart to the Lord,' she implores me, as though it's a simple thing to do.

'I'd rather open my legs to a man who can pay me in this life time,' I sneer. 'You ever done that, girl?'

The colour has drained from her skin, she looks at me as though I'm evil incarnate. 'Why is your heart so cold?' she asks, and then, pityingly she adds: 'I'll pray for your soul, we all will.'

'I want to leave,' I announce, slicing open an apple and offering half to her.

She looks at the apple, green peel scored deep and ringed with juice. 'You can't leave, not just yet anyway,' she says, taking the apple as though it's a peace offering. 'And I *will* pray for you,' she adds emphatically.

'Don't bother, my soul's beyond redemption.'

'I can't believe that,' she declares with a certainty that comes from not knowing what sort of a worthless bitch I am. Shit. This girl, and she can't be more than seventeen or eighteen, believes it all, she believes it deep down, right down in the heart of her cunt. That's why she's here of course. Paranoid scheming bitch that I am, I know that she's here to teach me by example. As though faith is something that's infectious, a viral strain passed from person to person. Fuck. I'd rather give her a dose of my own viral strain.

'If I picked this knife up and stabbed you with it, would you fight me?' I ask, toying with the blade because I can sense how uncomfortable it makes her.

'I wouldn't try to stab you back,' she tells me, hesitantly.

'Would you turn the other cheek?' I ask, smiling, bringing the knife up between us, turning it over in my hand so that the blade catches the sun and sends a beam of light tracking through the room.

'I wouldn't hurt you,' she assures me, eyes fixed on the blade glinting purposefully.

'Let me cut you then,' I suggest, reaching out with my other hand to grab hold of her wrist. She tenses but doesn't pull her arm away, instead she's fascinated by the play of light on steel.

'Why are you doing this?' she asks. 'Is this a test of faith?'

I laugh. She'd like that, I'm sure. A little test of faith, a drop of blood shed to prove her devotion to the Lord. 'Yes, a test of faith.' I hold her wrist tightly and then bring the knife down towards it. I can feel her pulse as it quickens, the blood racing through her veins as the adrenaline kicks in. Her pretty blue eyes are so wide, she looks pretty, a real turn on as those lashes stretch open with fear and horror. The knife touches her skin, cold steel blade stroking her warm flesh.

'Shall I?' I whisper, knuckles white against her wrist.

'There's no need,' she tells me, only I can tell that she's lying. She wants to be cut, she needs to feel the steel pierce her flesh, to watch the blood flow. She needs to feel this, she aches to be hurt so that her faith can come through with flying colours.

I dig the knife, a sharp, jagged movement. A cry of horror and the blood pours from my hand. I let it flow, let my blood pour over her trapped wrist. It hurts, sharp stinging pain but all I feel is satisfaction. Faith has been tested, and my pain is real.

'I'll get something to clear that up,' she says, finally snapping to life again. How disappointing for her, I can almost see it in her eyes.

'What the fuck does this prove?' I demand, releasing her arm. I position my hand carefully, letting the blood drip slowly, drop by bloody drop, onto the crinkled black leather of my jacket. It trails down slowly, staining my second skin with the stuff that flows inside me. It hurts and I'm glad, so fucking glad.

♦

I'm taken from my room along a corridor that leads to a flight of stairs heading down. I follow meekly, arm bandaged, looking forward to coming face to face with Sister Catherine. The thing that's most apparent is the quiet, the whole place is pervaded by an atmosphere of solitude and serenity. It's an unnatural quiet, but I guess it's the kind of atmosphere they try hard to maintain. It must be a big building, but I don't get much of a chance to look around, still it has the right air of tranquillity about it.

'I don't even know your name,' I say when we stop at the door to the office.

She looks startled. 'I am Sister Sarah,' she tells me as she knocks respectfully on the heavy wooden door.

I smile as she holds the door open for me to go in first. It's a big room and well illuminated by the light that streams in through two massive windows. A view of rolling, landscaped grounds but my eyes are drawn to the large canvas that hangs between the windows. Christ, tortured eyes turned up towards heaven, an expression of ecstatic agony on his face. His crown of thorns digs deep into waxy flesh, liberating jewels of thick, scarlet blood to trickle down his face. Behind him the clouds swirl and rage, grey explosions that are bubbling up from within the earth. But it's the pain that strikes me, the suffering in those sad brown eyes, the torment that he is enduring. It's a portrait but I can easily imagine the nails through his flesh, his body taut on the crucifix, blood snaking down to mingle with the mud at the foot of the cross.

I manage to turn my attention to the woman sitting at the heavy oak desk, under the canvas that dominates the room with such consummate ease. Mother Superior, Our Sister, Queen Bitch, she is all of these things and more. Cold eyes, grey as stone, a full, sensuous mouth, lips unadorned. Smooth white skin that is unblemished. She is dressed to type, black and white, her hair hidden by her cowl, body clothed in black, only her hands are visible. Long, elegant fingers adorned with silver and gold rings, long nails too, talons that are glossy but uncoloured. I look into her eyes and we understand each other, she knows all about me, she has the eyes of a whore.

'Remove the bandage,' she orders promptly, pointing to my wrist.

I undo the bandage and let it fall to the floor. I'm wearing my leather jacket, nothing she can do will frighten me. A smile of amusement crosses my face, but it's a smile that is not shared or returned.

Sister leans across the desk and grabs my wrist. She looks at the cut for a second, it's not very deep and is already scabbed up with dried blood. 'And what was this supposed to prove?' Sister demands of me, pushing my hand away.

I shrug. What the fuck was it supposed to prove? It felt like a good idea at the time, I wanted to see how Sarah, poor, frightened little Sarah, would react. 'I don't know,' I admit carelessly. 'Why does it have to prove anything?'

'Was it to prove that your lack of faith was as strong as her profession of faith?' Sister demands, eyeing Sarah with the same cold gaze she's using on me. 'Or did you want to prove the strength of your own faith?'

'She doesn't have any faith,' Sarah whispers. She's standing beside me, at the same level as me, as though we had engaged in some sinful, duplicitous act.

'But she does have faith,' Sister states firmly. 'She has an enviable faith in herself. She has pride in abundance, so much so that she has forgotten her obligations to our Lord.'

'Oh, shit,' I sigh, 'don't try and convert me, I'm not fucking interested.'

Sister looks at me and gives me an icy smile. 'How strong do you believe yourself to be?' she asks.

Another bored shrug. 'Can I go home?' I ask instead of replying.

'Do you think you're stronger than Sarah?'

I laugh. 'Of course I'm stronger than she is,' I tell her, turning to look at Sarah, who's staring resolutely at her feet, the epitome of weakness.

'Sarah has faith in the Lord, she is far stronger than you,' Sister tells me. She's a clever bitch because she knows I'll argue this point. I don't give a shit about religion, about belief or any of that crap, but she's talking about *me*.

'This is a stupid argument,' I respond, unable to stop my confusion from showing through.

'We can prove it. Very simply.'

I look at Sarah, who doesn't have the strength of will to look me in the face. Her pretty blue eyes are filled with tears, she's standing there so fucking weak and wishy washy. 'Prove it then,' I agree, inevitably.

Our Sister smiles, as though she has won already and I've lost just by agreeing to the test. Those eyes are filled with triumph. She sits back down behind the desk and opens one of the drawers. She reaches in and pulls out a whip, which she places on the blotter that sits in the middle of the desk. Short handle, thin leather strands that are knotted and braided. She smiles at me and then turns to Sarah. 'Undress.'

'Now?' Sarah whispers, appalled by the request.

'Now,' Sister confirms, 'and make sure you take off everything.'

I feel sort of sorry for Sarah, but I can't help smiling as she begins to nervously strip off. She looks good, face about to collapse into sobs, beautiful body about to be exposed. She could earn a fortune doing that little girl act on the streets. For a second I'm jealous but then I remember that this is supposed to be some sort of test. 'You've got her well trained,' I sneer sarcastically.

'She is stronger than you,' Sister tells me, 'as you'll soon see. It takes strength not to question, real strength, more strength than you'll ever possess.'

'No it doesn't,' I laugh. 'It takes strength to question everything. Any bitch can go with the flow, that's fucking easy.'

'Is it?' Again I get a smile from her, a teasing, taunting kind of smile. 'If it's so easy then use this on Sarah.'

I'm handed the whip, the long strands unfurling as it is handed over. Sarah is standing next to me, completely nude. A fringe of blonde hair barely covers her sex, prominent pussy lips are hidden behind nervous fingers. Small breasts with nipples that point away from each other, which she tries unsuccessfully to shield with her other hand. Her face is red, colouring brightly as she struggles to retain some sense of decorum. The pretty little slut is obviously uncomfortable, she can't wait to scuttle away and put her clothes on, but of course she won't. She has faith, which means the bitch will never disobey, never step out of line.

'Well?' Sister urges impatiently. 'Beat her for me. Use the whip on her, show me just how strong you are.'

I take the whip, gripping fingers around the ridges of the handle. It's heavier than expected and the long lashes dangle by my side. Do I really do this? What does it prove? I hesitate, torn by my desire to prove my strength and by my unwillingness to play the game. The smile on Queen Bitch's face is growing broader, she thinks she's won, she's enjoying my hesitation and doubt.

'Sarah, on your hands and knees,' Sister decides, pointing to the floor in front of my feet. Sarah obeys instantly, getting down onto all fours right in front of me. I can see the disquiet in her eyes, but she can't give voice to doubt. Long legs and a smooth back, her backside nicely rounded and I can see the folds of her sex most clearly. Her breasts sway slightly as she manoeuvres into place, meek and submissive and ready to receive the lash.

'What does this prove?' I demand, tightening my grip on the whip. My breathing is faster and deeper, I can't help but feel confused. That fucking bitch is smiling and it's driving me insane.

'Prove to me how strong you are. Beat Sarah, hurt her for me.'

I raise the whip and hold it there, high above my head. I grit my teeth and swing the whip down, the strands of leather whistle in unison and come down with a snap on Sarah's unblemished skin. She exhales slowly, as though breathing out the pain I have so casually imparted. Her back is red, I can see the individual lines marked by each of the strands of the whip. I raise the whip again and bring it down, just as hard, on her lower back. A snap of leather on flesh, Sarah tensed up, red welts raised on her pale skin.

'Is that enough?' I ask, looking to Sister Catherine for an answer.

She shakes her head. 'You've hardly touched her. I want you to show how strong you are, not how merciful.'

I raise the whip again, doing my best not to think about what I'm doing. Whip held high, balanced motionlessly for a moment and then it's slicing through the air. It bites, this time Sarah gasps and moves forward involuntarily. Bitch, it fucking hurts! Again. I raise the whip and beat it down on her bare back, cutting into the flesh of her lower back and upper thighs. I see the red tracks, lattice lines cut into her flesh. Again, I want her to cry, I want her to scream. Again. A steady rhythm, whistle through the air and then the snap as it cuts into her. Hurt, you bitch! Fucking scream for me! I swap hands, use my left to cut her across the shoulders, the leather splayed out as it lands viciously. In moments her skin is patterned red and pink, droplets of blood like fissures on her flesh. But she remains silent and in place.

'Happy now?' I demand, throwing the whip to the floor. I can't do it any more, I can't hurt Sarah. It's not just her, it's not Sarah in particular, I just can't beat someone for no reason. My heart is pounding and for the first time I realise that I'm shaking.

'So weak,' Sister remarks sadly, shaking her head with disappointment. 'How many strokes did you last? Ten, a dozen?'

'I hit her, didn't I?'

'No, you felt sorry for her. Sarah feels sorry for you too, of course, but she's stronger than you are. Undress,' she orders.

'Sarah's turn now, is it?' I laugh, convinced that Sarah's not going to be able to go through with this. I slip my jacket off and let it fall into a crumpled heap on the floor. The gown I pull off over my head and I'm naked. My nipples are bruised and sore when I touch them and I'm not sure why. Again I'm certain that there's something I should know but I can't reach it.

'How's this?' I sneer and bend over the desk and part my thighs. It's a lewd, open position, offering my backside and a view of my cunt to poor innocent Sarah. She can hardly look, her face is as red as the scars on her back, as though she feels the shame I should be feeling. Good, I want the bitch to take a good long look at me, at this body men pay to fuck. This is it, girl, this is what a man wants: a willing body, open, available, ready.

'Sarah,' Sister tells her sternly, 'this sinful child has no shame. She flaunts her body and yet does not understand the significance of her nakedness. Teach her, let her feel the pain so that she might understand. Scourge her flesh so that the soul might be purified.'

Sarah picks the whip up off the floor, holding it gingerly, afraid that somehow it's going to strike her of its own accord. Long strands of leather that swish together as she toys with it, her fingers coiling around the handle still warm with my sweat. She avoids looking me in the eyes, which makes me smile and wiggle my backside like a naughty little slut.

The first strike on my flesh is unexpected, the sharp daggers of pain shooting all over my back. It's not what I expected, but it's something I can endure without problem. I listen for the tell-tale swish and then brace myself for the second stroke against my flesh. So sharp, it stings and smarts where the knotted leather bites into me with wicked glee. I look over my shoulder, hoping to catch Sarah's eye, certain that she won't be able to carry on once we make contact. The first few strokes are easy, there's the anger to get you through it, anger that you've been conned into playing this stupid game.

I gasp as the whip bites deeper, I can feel it cutting my skin, scoring long lines into my back. Sarah is hurting me, putting all her strength into this one task. Her nipples are bulging and her breasts sway as she brings the whip down hard. I listen to the whistle as it slices cleanly through the air, tensing myself for the impact which strikes so hard. The sound of it fills the room, a steady crack crack crack of leather and flesh. My breathing is faster now, and I'm squirming. Fucking bitch... Sarah's hurting me...

'Don't stop now,' Sister Catherine spurs her servant on, the cold steel in her voice echoing the sharpest edges of the pain.

I start to rise, unable to take any more but my hands are seized by the Sister, whose sharp nails dig into my flesh. Her face is so close to mine, I can feel her breath on my lips. Our eyes meet and we understand each other, her mouth is set, lips closed firmly, cruelly. She wants to make me suffer, and the bitch is the sort that gets exactly what she wants, always.

'Sarah... Stop!' I hiss as the whip continues to play on me. There's fire on my back, the pain seething and bubbling on my skin and then seeping deep within me. I struggle but am held down, stretched against this cold wooden desk so that the lash can cut deep. My nipples are sore as they brush against the blotter and the smooth polished surface of the desk.

Sarah ignores my cries, there is no mercy here, she's hurting me for my own good. I cry out now, unable to hold back as the whip draws blood. I can feel it, droplets of red that merge with each other, turning into fluid runs that lie parallel to my ribs. I struggle hard, try to lash out with my feet but I am stretched across the desk, the sharp edges pressing into my waist.

There's a momentary pause, I breathe again, hoping that Sarah has relented, but I'm wrong of course. Wishful thinking, Sarah is driven by her faith, my cries and complaints are nothing to her. She recommences, stepping back to swing the whip low and hard. I scream as the lashes bite into my thighs and buttocks. Again and again, she wields the whip with a quiet fury that shows no signs of abating. My backside is quivering and the tears stream down my face. The bitch won't stop! Pain, wave after wave of pain, cutting fine red lines into my body. I'm trembling, weak, unresisting, naked body oozing with spikes of blood and traced with thin red lines, a road map of my punishment.

Our Sister releases me and I slip to the floor, falling heavily at

Sarah's feet. There's no let up. The Lord shows no mercy to the unrepentant sinner, and a bitch like me is always unrepentant. Sarah is astride, standing over my body, oblivious to her own nakedness now that she is charged with the holiest of tasks. I try to crawl away, hoping to escape her somehow. She swings the whip down hard and it catches me across the chest, individual thongs cutting at the soft, tender flesh of my breasts. I scream and fall flat on my face. Down again, hard and vicious. My body is wracked with pain, and yet there is excitement too, as though the liquid pain that surges inside me incites some spark of aphrodisiac excitement.

I inch along the floor, clawing my way in an effort to escape the singing, stinging cry of the whip. When I turn I look into Sarah's eyes I'm frightened. There's no mercy there, no love, all that I see is a febrile excitement, a physical, sexual desire that she expresses so eloquently with the whip. I scream suddenly, shriek my pain so that my throat burns and chest strains. It's a scream of defeat, capitulation, the fucking bitch has won, I can't take any more.

'Go to your room, now,' Sister Catherine tells me. 'I will speak with you later.'

She is standing in front of me, black boots poking out from her black vestment. She extends a toe, offers it to me with a sly smile. Does she really want me to make this gesture? Sarah has stepped back, out of breath, her body tinged pink with excitement, nipples harder than they've ever been.

'You know what to do,' I'm told.

My body is alive with sharp twitches and daggers of pain, I'm trembling uncontrollably. I barely have the power to move. I reach out slowly and touch my lips to the cool, polished leather. This bitch will hurt me, and we both know it.

FIVE

Eyes staring into darkness. Eyes filled with panic, darting nervously, the eyes of a frightened animal. A buzz of sensation, white noise that fills the void. Blood rushing in my ears, pulsing with the heightened heart beat that pounds my chest. Frightened eyes straining to see in the darkness. Something's going to happen and I pull and pull to break free without knowing or understanding what's happening.

I scream behind the gag, eyes bulging wet with tears as the pain burns through me. A white poker that burns behind the eyes. Body taut as I pull, struggling like an animal, muscles tight, bundles of fibre fit to explode. There is no escape, the frame of the bed creaks and groans as I try to throw myself free. I have to get away, I have to cut loose from this pain that burns through me. I scream and scream and nothing comes out, nothing but spit and snot. Breathing hard, breathing hard, afraid that I'm going to black out again.

The pain subsides, the pure intensity cutting out. Body released from the electric surge that cuts my flesh as I struggle against the bonds that hold me down. Body aches, trembling, shaking, hurting. Hurting, hurting, hurting so that everything else is blocked out. I cannot think, cannot see, cannot do anything but feel. Eyes, bloodshot and soaked, stare into nothing, searching desperately for a way out. I am an animal, trapped and chained, sacrificed for reasons I do not understand.

It's going to happen again, the fear grows inside me. I fight, pulling hard though every movement cuts into bruised and bloodied flesh. I cannot scream, my nose is blocked so I can hardly breath. When will this end? No warning. The pain cuts through me, fucking me deep in the head as it surges through my cunt. I cannot take this, I cannot take this. Kill me, please fucking kill me put me out of this fucking misery.

It subsides, falling away like the ebb tide of the ocean dragging across the sand. Sweat and piss soak my body, blood pounding in my ears. Doctor and Nurse, clinicians of science, angels of mercy, stand at my side to minister to my needs. Cunt lips open, clamped by metal jaws which spew out pure electric current.

'Is she ready, Doctor?' Nurse asks, barely even glancing at my tortured, bloodied body. I am nothing but meat, naked flesh stripped of dignity and control.

Doctor considers his opinion and nods appreciatively. He steps forward, looks into my empty eyes, checks to see that there's nothing there. I am empty, everything human has been shocked to smithereens. He smiles to me, he is happy with what he sees. I am his creation, his living corpse to play with.

I can barely move, so weak, so helpless. Legs are strapped apart, soaked with my own stale piss. Cunt lips clamped open and bleeding. Nurse has no hesitation or doubt. Practised fingers, protected by antiseptic gel and a thin layer of latex. She takes something hard and phallic and forces it tightly between my arse cheeks, forcing her instrument deep into my rectal passage.

Panic rising again, my body tries to fight the anal probe as it is forced into me. Doctor smiles and unzips his trousers. Flaccid cock sprays hot, steaming piss into my face and hair. Piss washes with my tears, into my eyes and along my lips, soaking hair

*matted with spit and sweat. He pisses good and long, leisurely
emptying his bladder over me.*

*It surges through me again, current so pure and strong it blots
everything else out. Fire behind eyes that feel like they're about
to explode. It travels, arcing through my body from my cunt
through to my brain. Dildo shoved up my arse is gripped tight as
I squirm and scream, trying desperately to find oblivion. It hurts.
I hurt, I hurt. Why can't I die?*

I wake up, bathed in sweat, breathing hard. It feels so real, the
echoes of it tingling between my thighs. I'm wet, cunt soaked
ready for fucking. Nightmare or memory? I can't be sure, I can't
be sure. Shaking hands and pounding heart, I stare up into
space and offer thanks that I can move and breath freely.

I look round and find Sister Catherine, looking Godly and
superior, sitting by my bed. There's no concern in her eyes, she
knows what the score is even if I don't.

I close my eyes and try hard to regain control of my breathing.
The nightmare images are gone now, banished by the mere fact
of her presence. What does she want with me? Wasn't the
beating I suffered enough for her? I feel anger swelling up inside
me, growing like an erection until it's hard and lethal. I want to
lash out, to destroy her and her sick world.

'Is this how you get your kicks?' I hiss through gritted teeth.
'Watching little girls having bad dreams?'

'Is that how you think of yourself, as a little girl?' she asks,
obvious amusement displayed in the square formed by her veil,
a box that hides hair and neck, leaving a rectangular panel for
her expressions to form and break at will.

'Where's your real little girl?' I respond instantly. 'Where's little
Sister Sarah?'

'She at least knows her place,' I'm reminded. 'It would serve you well to remember yours.'

'Which is where, exactly?' I ask, as if I don't already know.

'I'll not dignify that with an answer,' I'm told haughtily.

I sigh, too tired and disturbed to offer any further resistance. 'What do you want with me?'

'I want to help you,' I'm told simply. There's no sign that she's talking crap, this is the sort of woman who never lies. Dishonesty is never as brutal as the plain unvarnished truth, and I just know that brutality is the kick that drives this bitch.

'How the fuck are you going to do that?'

'I'm going to help you discover the truth that lies inside you,' she explains. 'Your soul is still pure, even if your body is corruption itself. There are questions that you are asking and I will help you to the answers.'

'Why me?'

'That's a stupid question,' I'm told firmly but not unreasonably.

'Why me?' I persist. 'Why am I here? Was I picked deliberately or what?'

'It's still a stupid question,' Our Sister replies. 'If there is a master plan do you think you'd ever be privy to it? If the universe has a Maker do you think you'd ever be in a position to have knowledge of it?'

'And if there's nothing? If the universe is a random fuck up of a thing?' I ask earnestly, feeling empty inside because I know that's the answer that's true.

'Then we're all lost souls, there is no hope for any of us.'

'That's the truth, isn't it?' I whisper, looking into her icy eyes for confirmation of the one fact that I know is true. The universe doesn't give a fuck, we're nothing, I'm nothing, you're nothing. It means fuck all whether we live or die. If you live then it's pain and suffering until you die. Until you die. Then what?

'You have the chance, now, here. Do you know what is real? Do you understand what is holy? Pain,' she tells me, stating the only fact we're ever likely to agree on. 'Pain is the only reality. Master it, learn from it, accept it. Do you see what chance you have here?'

'Is that why I'm here?' I ask quietly, unable to shake off the feeling that I'm here for a reason. Fuck it, is it chance that has brought me this far? I can't believe that the random universe would conspire to deliver me here, to hand me over to *her* without some reason. Of all the whores in the world, of all the worthless bitches that walk the streets at night, why me?

'You've so much to learn,' she smiles.

'Fucking tell me!' I demand, angered by her pretend mysteries. I'm sick of her fucking enigmatic bitch routine, it's pissing me off. I don't want it any more, I don't want to play this game.

'Obedience is the first lesson you must learn,' she tells me coldly. 'Obedience and humility. You think too much of yourself, you value yourself too highly. Do I have to remind you that you're a cheap whore, that your body and soul are bought and sold with loose change?'

I laugh bitterly. 'Is that it? I'm a whore so I'm worth nothing. Some fucking charitable religion you've got,' I laugh derisively.

She stands up, eyes cold with disdain. 'I think you do need

reminding of how little your sordid little life is worth. Do you really understand how hopeless your condition is? You have been committed here, into my personal custody. If I so desire I will return you to the hospital where your torments may begin again. You have an infinite capacity to suffer, there are a million ways to hurt, do you really wish to experience them all? Or else I'll send you on to the compound, where your existence will be worth less than the existence of the beasts in the fields.'

'I just want to *know*,' I respond vehemently, trying to express the deepest, most important need that exists inside me. I know I'm a worthless bitch, a cheap slut destined to die in misery with a knife in my guts and a cock up my arse, but I'm still me. Me, fuck it and not some other bitch.

She looks at me for at moment, practised eyes measuring up. 'Were you excited by your dream?' she asks, switching tact with barely a flicker of emotion. She knows the answer, it was more of a statement than a question.

Was I excited? Visions of electrocution, torture without escape, pain without measure. 'No,' I reply, avoiding her questing eyes. Fuck, how could I be? How could I be turned on by a dream of senseless torture? The pain lives on, as though it's a memory and not just a nightmare, as though I have really lived and suffered every moment of its agony.

She pulls the blanket back, making me curl up instantly as the cold air attacks my nakedness. Is my back still scored deep by the whip? I remember the pain as Sarah beat me, hitting me with the whip in a rhythm that left no room for doubt or hesitation. Faith, that's what it is, and my lack of it is evidenced by the cuts and welts that score the white flesh of my back.

A slap across the face, quick and hard, and I stop struggling. She knows what she's looking for and she's not about to take any modesty shit from a street slut like me. Her fingers reach down,

down between my thighs to seek out the wetness that will betray me. Of course I'm wet, stupid fucking bitch that I am, worthless whore beneath contempt, I'm turned on by my dream of electrical torture. My cunt is soaked just as my nipples are erect, and her holy fingers press deep into my cunt to prove it.

'The body betrays the spirit,' she murmurs, digging her fingers into my cunt as though gouging eyes from a skull. 'The body betrays the spirit, which is why we must mortify the flesh. Suffering is holy, it feeds the spirit and cleanses the body.'

He fingers are digging into the soft, sensitive membranes of my pussy, sharp nails digging violently into my cunt. I gasp, clutching at the side of the bed as the pain merges with the wet pleasure inside me. 'That hurts,' I whisper feebly, afraid of the violence that I sense this woman is capable of. Her eyes are evil, ice cold and knowing, she frightens me and she knows it.

'You'll help me,' she says, 'you have an instinctive understanding of the unity of pleasure and pain. Your flesh is strong and your spirit weak, but I will change that. And it will be instructive to all who witness it.'

I'm squirming, trying to inch away from her invading fingers. She clamps down on my clit, piercing me with a lightning jolt of sensation that takes me back into my nightmare. I can see it now, strapped down, leather biting into my limbs, body swathed in stinking sweat, my arse clamped tight around a massive dildo as the current courses through me. And there, at the epicentre, as the livid electric sensation is at its strongest, I am screaming my climax. I come and I come, body rigid with shock and pleasure, suffering the little death which is a promise of the future.

'You'll help me with Sarah, first,' she adds, thinking out loud. She removes her hand from between my thighs but I dare not relax. Pussy soaked fingers are brought to my mouth, hovering near my lips expectantly. I can breathe the essence of my sex, the liquid pleasure secreted from the deepest part of me. I lick her fingers slowly, tasting myself, coating my tongue from her long, elegant fingers. It lingers in my mouth, the forbidden taste of my own cunt, and then I swallow it down. I don't stop, I lick her fingers and then take them into my mouth, swirling my tongue around and around, caressing them as well as cleaning them.

She slaps me again, wet fingers stinging my face. 'Do you think you seduce me?' she demands wearily.

'I just want to please you,' I whimper like an abject little bitch. I'm frightened. Of her. Of me.

She stands up suddenly and gathers the long black habit around her waist. Before I have a chance to object she is astride me, sitting on my chest with her back to my face. Her black garment is spread about her, covering my chest in its rough, loose folds. I can feel her warmth against my nakedness, the soft heat of her sex pressed between my breasts, her knees pressed into my sides, feet clad in sandals holding my head still.

'I am an angel of the Lord,' she tells me, speaking imperiously from atop her human throne. 'There is no mercy in this house, there is only fear, obedience and pain. You will serve or be sacrificed, there is no other way.'

I hesitate. 'What if I refuse?' I ask, pinned down and unable to move. My heart is pounding and I know she can feel it in her cunt, little tremors that snake from my chest to her clit. I have to ask, no matter how weak or vulnerable, I have to ask, I have to make some gesture of denial.

She looks down at me, dead eyes without feeling. 'To refuse means you have a choice. You have no option, you are dead to the world, you have ceased to exist. Sacrifice or service?'

I close my eyes and the words sink in, seeping into my brain like acid eating at my flesh. She's right, I am dead to the world, another cheap whore gone missing from the streets. Who will grieve me? Who will mourn my loss?

Her skirts are lifted slowly, revealing soft pale skin, long thighs of smooth glassy flesh. She moves back slowly, covering my face with the folds of material that deny her body until there is a warm darkness about me. I can barely see but I know that her backside is above me, her pussy lips close to my mouth. This is my opportunity to serve, to use my body to give her pleasure. What a pure, evil bitch she is, she knows that my cunt is wet with desire, she knows my mind is dead with despair.

I press my mouth to her body, kissing softly the underside of her thigh, my face brushing against the coarse curls of her sex. I breathe her female scent the way I breathed my own earlier, and I know that her taste will mingle with my own. She is squatting over me, balanced above me, confident in her power over me.

I tease the folds of her sex with my tongue, opening the hidden bloom of her femininity so that I might seek out the nectar of her desire. I toy with her pussy lips, licking them, biting very gently to give her pleasure that is denied me. She squats lower, opening herself more as my movements grow in strength and urgency. I press my tongue into her sex, forcing my mouth into her cunt so that I can kiss her deeply. I lick and suck, explore the recesses of her cunt as far as I can. She's wet, her essence filling my mouth as I tongue her forcefully.

Her pussy bud is throbbing, a nub of pure pleasure that I begin to tease playfully. The first moans of her pleasure are muffled by the loose folds of her habit, but I hear enough to be certain that I am serving her well. I begin to bite her clit, to force waves of pleasure to pass through her body and to be echoed back to me as a deluge of pussy juice. I lose myself, concentrating only on pleasuring her cunt, in using mouth and lips, teeth and tongue to give her pleasure. She is thrashing wildly, her knees digging into me as she rides my mouth hard. I can hardly breathe, all I can do is swallow her pussy juice and work my mouth against the centre of her being.

She climaxes, arching her back as she forces herself down on my mouth. I feel suffocated under her, my face trapped between her thighs. My own pussy is aching for her touch, my clitty throbbing with a desire so strong I'm on the edge of orgasm. She is breathing hard as my tongue laps slowly, playfully with her pussy lips again. My face is smeared with her juices, and every breath I take is scented by her. I want to touch myself, to give myself the pleasure I have given to her, yet I am afraid of her reaction.

She moves forward an inch and I imagine she is about to get up. I relax, hoping that she is going to return to her room so that I can steal my own pleasure. Fuck, I long to press my fingers into my cunt, to frig myself like a dirty bitch until I scream my orgasm into a pillow.

'And here, also,' she tells me, showing me by placing a finger against her tight rear hole, only inches from my mouth.

Jesus. I can hardly believe what this fucking bitch wants. I feel revolted, the horror rises up like a bilious explosion from the pit of my stomach. I'm not doing that, there's no fucking way I'm going to lick her arsehole. The bitch, all that fucking holiness shit and she's just a warped, sick whore like any other.

'I've sucked your cunt!' I complain, trying to turn away from her. She's sitting back down, squatting over me again. Knees dig painfully into my sides, hurting me more and more.

'Do it!' she seethes through gritted teeth. 'You'll do anything I tell you to do, without exception. Now, do as I say!'

The curves of her backside press against my face, her arse-cheeks splayed so that her anal hole is stretched tight. I can't do it, I can't bring myself to lick her there. I gasp as she digs me with her knees, as though I'm a stubborn animal. But what bitch would ask this of an animal? Lower than that, I'm a piece of shit so I should have no problem licking her shit hole.

Sharp nails dig into my thigh, digging down so that there's a tight ball of pain that makes me want to scream. She draws blood, I can feel it pouring where she's pierced my skin. I can't do it! A sharp red explosion of pain, her nails cut me again, digging violently into my thigh.

I press my tongue against her anal hole, press it hard so that I feel the ring of muscle resisting. No more explosions of pain, only the smarting and the sting where she scratched my skin away. No fucking choice, I do as commanded because that is what I am here for.

I lick back and forth between her buttocks, caressing her rear cleavage with my tongue, wetting her in preparation. Wetness dribbles from her sex and I lick that up too, every drop. Her backside is tight, each time I stop and lick around the dark anal ring she murmurs softly with unrestrained pleasure. Soon I am poking my tongue into her behind, pressing against the wetted anal ring and deep into her rectum. The sounds of her pleasure increase, her soft moans of delight growing deeper as I tongue her arsehole more vigorously. I do not stop, no longer revolted by what I am doing I find my own desire growing stronger.

My fingers travel along the smoothness of her thighs, caressing her lovingly as she sits astride my mouth. I stroke the inside of her thigh, my fingers pressing firmly against her flesh, revelling in the softness of her skin. My face is pressed hard under her backside and when she lifts herself slightly I lift my head also. She is beside herself with pleasure, moaning and gasping as I touch and kiss her. My fingers find her sex but she slaps my hand away, instead she begins to stroke her own clit in time with the thrusts of my tongue into her anal passage. I worship her arsehole, I cannot go deep enough. I'm not worthy enough to touch her sex with my fingers, I may give pleasure only with my mouth.

I climax suddenly, brought to orgasm by this, the most debased of acts. My mouth is glued to her anus, my tongue paying homage to the dark orifice as though it is a shrine be worshipped. I see myself, lying flat on my back deliriously tonguing another woman's arsehole and I am filled with disgust and desire in equal measure. The disgust drives me over the edge, gives my orgasm an intensity which makes me shudder bodily.

Her climax is screamed in ecstasy, her fingers in her cunt and my tongue up her arsehole. She grinds herself down on my mouth, so that it feels like she is fucking me with her anal hole. Her pussy juice is smeared over my chin and mouth, a layer of bodily fluid that I long to lick clean.

In a moment she is standing by the bed, looking serene and thoroughly composed again. Her eyes sparkle and her face is flushed slightly, but other than that there is no sign of the dark pleasure she has just experienced. I feel like I've been orally raped, as though she has taken my mouth and fucked it viciously. I can taste her cunt and the dark cloying flavour of her behind, the tastes of her body suffuse my mouth and tongue.

'Do you see how weak you are?' she asks me, with only the faintest tremor in her voice.

I am still breathing hard, dazed, not a little confused by what has occurred. 'Didn't you like it?' I ask quietly, eyes filling with tears I do not want.

'Don't you see?' she demands angrily. 'You were forced to serve and yet you found pleasure in it. Is there nothing you would not do?'

'I don't understand,' I protest weakly. 'I'm bad because I enjoyed what I was forced to do? If I hadn't found pleasure in it, that would have made me good?'

She looks at me for a moment, coldly calculating her response. 'There is still so much for you to learn,' she warns. 'Tomorrow we begin in earnest. You will suffer, of that I am certain, but perhaps you will also finally find the path to the truth which has so far eluded you.'

'Why do I have to suffer?' I ask. My eyes are closed and I can sense the darkness that this woman exudes, a black aura of evil that masquerades as holy goodness. What I can't work out is whether she believes what she's saying or whether she's just a clever bitch getting her way.

'Because suffering is the essence of being human,' she announces with a tone of utter certainty. She speaks with an executioner's voice, pronouncing sentence from which there is no escape.

There's nothing for me to say. I feel tired, exhausted mentally and physically. I don't want to think any more, I don't want to have questions circling endlessly in my head. I want to finger fuck myself to sleep, I want to drift from bodily pleasure into a dark and dreamless sleep.

Sister leaves, her long black habit swishing softly as she walks. I can't relax however, my body has its demands, my cunt aches and my nipples beg, the blood rushing in my veins screams in my ears. I want to sleep but know that to get there I have to bring myself to orgasm first.

There is no time, the door opens a moment after the dark angel has gone. Another Sister is here, older than Sarah, her face a mask that I cannot read. That she is here on orders is not in doubt, she moves with the swift efficiency of a practised minion.

'Why don't you just leave me alone?' I complain wearily.

'This is for your own good,' comes the reply, as though there is the possibility of some other reply and this one was chosen from the infinity of alternatives. Things that hurt are always for our own good, it has to be an iron law of a universe so perverse it loathes our existence with a passion that is immeasurable and unknowable.

I say nothing. Instead I submit, complete capitulation. My arms are strapped together and my hands pulled high above my shoulder. A steel chain is threaded through the head of the bed and is then connected to cuffs on my wrists. My legs are parted and each ankle secured to a corner of the bed. Stretched tight, there is barely room to move. The ache in my sex will be unfulfilled, the desire will burn its embers through the darkness, robbing me of sleep and strength.

'What if I want to piss?' I ask, rather too meekly for it to be interpreted as resistance.

My jailer looks at me and smiles grimly. 'Then you'll soak in it until the morning,' she tells me warmly.

It's the answer I would have given in her place.

SIX

It was agony, suffered through the long hours of the night and into the chill dawn which found me still awake. I had not slept, rather I had lingered in that dead zone between sleep and reality. My body ached, stretched unnaturally so that every muscle seemed to scream its own song of pain. At times I was physically numb, or else my body fought the chains as bouts of cramp attacked me like demons in the night. My mind was in turmoil, haunted by images that were part memory, part fantasy and part hallucination. I didn't know what the fuck was going on. And all the time words echoed in my mind: *suffering is the essence of humanity, pain is the only reality, why me?, why me?*

I couldn't concentrate, when I tried to piece together the sequence of events that had conspired to send me here, to this house of pain, it made no sense. Fuck it, life is shit but I had always imagined that it made sense in a sick, distorted kind of way. Now where was I? Nothing made sense and the only thing I could be sure of was pain and pleasure. A weird pairing but they were always there, together, melded, welded until I didn't know where one began and the other ended.

When the first light began to sneak through the window I knew that the new day would be worse then the last. Every day from here on would be worse, harder, more painful, more extreme. Where would it fucking end? Shit, the thought frightened me and the more I tried to fight it the more it took hold.

I wanted to piss, I felt swollen, bladder maliciously conspiring to find moisture even though my mouth was as dry as a pre-pubescent cunt. I was stretched open, ankles tied to each corner of the bed and that made it worse. I ached to piss, I wanted to be released from the burden of holding it in but there was no fucking way I was going to give those bitches the pleasure. I wouldn't soak in it. Our Sister, Sister Catherine, the queen bitch herself, was right. Pride. I fucking still had some, where I had no right to any. Shit doesn't have pride.

At last the darkness through the window turned into a greyish light, a washed out light without the power to transform the day into something sweet. Grey and miserable and yet I was filled with a strange sense of wonder as I watched the day unfold, the light appearing beyond the horizon that I could just about see from the window. Grey and miserable but still a new day. For a moment the searing thoughts were stilled and I felt an emotion I had thought myself incapable of. A new day and I felt a twinge of hope, astounded by the way the clouds rolled forward, waves of thick, delicious grey unfurling as the world swept forward. O stupid bitch that I am, I watch the dawn and feel something stir inside me.

The door opens and the moment is gone. How could it have lasted? Do I really imagine that the seed of hope could flower, blossoming into something real inside me? I want to scream at myself for having such pathetic illusions. This isn't me. I am strapped to a bed, arms pulled over my shoulders and legs pulled apart. Ready to be fucked. Ready to be beaten. Ready for anything but hope.

Our Sister, gracious and deadly, sweeps into the room, followed meekly by Sarah. Both dressed in black, holy vestments that obscure the fact that they are women like any other. And there I am. Naked and open, no denying my femininity, no missing

---

the cunt lips slightly parted, the shock of pubic hair and nipples so hard from the cold.

'Please...' I whisper, looking not at Sister Catherine but at Sarah, 'I'm going to die. Help me, please?'

And there are tears in my eyes. All night I've suffered and now I don't want to any more. I want to be held. I want to be touched and cuddled and loved. Treat me as a person, that's all I want and I'm crying because that's so little to ask for but I know I won't get it. I don't even have the energy for anger any more.

Sarah looks from me to Sister Catherine, looking for instructions because she's too fucking scared to move without being told. And that's where I'm going, that's how I'm going to be. All I want is what Sarah wants: to be treated right. She's handed herself over, she's renounced her very being so that she can get it. I can go the same way, so easily, we all can.

'Untie her,' is the instruction. Delivered without emotion, in that cold voice that sounds as though it has been stripped of all that is vital.

Sarah smiles to me, now that she is allowed to. My arms are released first, untied and the cuffs removed. It hurts like hell as the feeling returns to flesh so numb and cold it is ready for amputation. I rub my arms trying to press away the pain and to warm myself up at the same time.

'I've got to go to the toilet,' I whisper urgently, sitting forward as Sarah looks at the constraints that bind my ankles.

'What?' Sister Catherine demands, seizing on my words as though I have just confessed to some hideously mortal sin.

I swallow, dry throat rasping. 'I need to have a piss,' I tell her, eyes still watery with tears.

'Sarah, bring that glass,' Sister Catherine orders, waving an arm in the general direction of the jug and empty glass that have been tantalisingly close throughout the night.

I can see what's coming and I shake my head. No. I'm not going to do this. Not this. 'Don't do this, please...' I beg Sarah, looking into her frightened eyes in the hope that somehow we can connect, that somehow I'll give her the courage to resist. But there's no chance, to resist is to claim herself back and she doesn't want that.

'Today is the day you'll learn what it is to obey,' Sister Catherine tells me, reminding me of the promise she made the day before. I know what obedience means, it means handing yourself over, denying yourself. Slaves obey. Sluts obey. Except me. You buy my obedience, you never get it willingly.

Sarah is standing by my side, red faced with shame as she clasps the glass to her chest. She obeys like a good little girl should, even when she doesn't want to. No, fuck it, especially when she doesn't want to.

'Hold the glass for her,' Our Sister orders her.

I am hauled up onto my knees, my feet still chained to the bed. Sarah doesn't know what to do, she still hasn't worked out what's going on. On hands and knees, legs parted, in position but there's no way I'm going to play this game. I can feel the piss inside me, a wet bulge that I'm keeping to myself as though it's something precious.

'Hold the glass between her thighs,' is the next instruction. Sarah, horrified, obeys without question. The cold glass is pressed between my thighs, the lip of glass pressing against my cunt lips.

'Now you may relieve yourself,' Sister Catherine tells me, with all the natural generosity of spirit one expects from the pious.

'And now you can go fuck yourself,' I tell her, in the same spirit.

'Is that supposed to anger me?' she asks, unimpressed.

'I don't give a shit what you think,' I reply. The glass is pressed harder, like a hungry mouth waiting to feed from my cunt.

'This is so tiresome,' the queen bitch sighs. She moves behind me, the faint swish of her dark vestments masking the sound of her footsteps.

'You going to spank me?' I laugh. 'That's so fucking nasty, so fucking...'

I gasp as she pushes her middle finger through the tight anal ring, penetrating deep into my rectum. The pain is intense as my arsehole's so dry and I wasn't ready for her. She presses hard, pushing her finger deeper and deeper into my behind. It hurts and my gasps of discomfort fill the silence. The pressure in my bladder feels so much more intense, but I close my eyes and do my best to hold it in. The evil bitch, Jesus, the evil bitch. She removes her finger and then plunges it in again, fucking me harder in the arsehole. And then a second finger, really stretching my sphincter as I am anally penetrated.

'Do it,' whispers Sarah to me, knowing that it is pointless to resist.

I'm gasping and moaning. I'm wet, there's no way I can stop myself, no way I can hold back. My nipples are hardening too, there's a tightness in my belly and my breath is staggered. I arch my back, offering my arsehole to her, giving myself to her rapacious fingers. She can have me. She can fuck me. Sodomise me. Hurt me. I'm getting off on the pain and the humiliation and she knows it.

Her fingers are shoved into my mouth. I suck, greedily, licking the fingers that are still warm from being fucked into my anal hole. I suck and lick and take pleasure in it, not caring any more. O Jesus, why did it have to be this way?

I scream. Her nails draw blood from my nipple, claws sinking into the fount of human milk and kindness. Not milk, she draws blood wherever she touches, vampiric mother that she is. The sudden flash of pain makes me scream and the piss pours from my cunt. Torrents of it, hissing wet and warm from my cunt. It feels good, so very good and dirty. I'm panting and my pussy's aflame and I can't even put it out with all that piss. It fills the glass and then I feel it sliding down, dripping all over the place, coursing down my thighs in warm rivulets and ripples.

I look up, shocked by what I have done. Sarah is aghast, she holds a wet glass full of yellow piss as though it's going to explode in her hand. Her fingers are soaked through, droplets of piss dapple her skin. I think she's going to be sick.

Sister Catherine takes Sarah's pissed stained fingers and brings them to my lips. I look up at them, meekly, submissively. I have done that which I swore I wouldn't. Now I have to face the consequences, pay the price for pissing like an animal. I lick the dew drops of piss from Sarah's trembling hand. I taste the sharp, acidic taste of my piss, tingling on my tongue. I swallow the droplets down, cleaning her hand of the wetness that has soiled it. Shameless, I lick and lick, seeking out more of my piss so that I can savour it.

The glass is offered to me, the sides still dripping fluid that looks so innocent and yet I pissed it out of myself. My lips are closed but when the glass is pressed against them I take a sip of warm piss. I hold it there for a moment, a mouthful of piss, ready to spit it out in a gesture of rebellion. I swallow, take another sip

---

Pan Panziarka

and swallow.

'You too, Sarah,' I hear Sister Catherine say.

The glass is offered to other lips. Sarah's face is burning, self combusting with shame and degradation. She opens her mouth and takes a sip of my yellow water, she swallows and I see the revulsion rising up from the pit of her stomach. I think she's going to puke, but then faith is stronger than that. She drinks again, deeper, swallowing more of it, gulping down half a glass of my fresh piss.

'Share it,' we are told. Our tormentor in chief is evidently happy with our unquestioning obedience, her eyes sparkle with pleasure. Do we suck her arsehole again too? If she gathers up her robes I know that I'll do as she bids. I'll tongue her without hesitation, sticking my tongue into her rectum with a love that was entirely absent when she invaded my backside with her dead fingers.

I take a mouthful of piss and hold it there, waiting. Reluctantly Sarah moves towards me, our lips meet and I let the piss pour from my mouth to hers. I'm pissing it again, squirting it from my mouth into hers as though she had her mouth to my cunt. Mouth, cunt, anus. What's the difference?

I'm so fucking turned on. In moments Sarah and I are sharing long, searching kisses soaked with piss. It's all over my face and in my hair, I'm soiled, filthy and so aroused I'm sure I'm going to come. There's none left, the glass is dry and I want more. I want to kiss Sarah, I want to have her mouth on mine, to share the feelings of desire and disgust that are mingled in my confusion.

'Enough. Release her ankles now,' Our Sister tells Sarah, putting a stop to the sensual scene that unfolds before her. We've demeaned ourselves, that's where it ends for her. The filthy consummation of our submission, defiled and degraded, is all that she desires, our own wishes and desires count for nothing.

I am released, at last. I feel disgusted with myself, and yet immensely excited. My mouth is suffused with the taste of my piss, I can feel it inside me, as if my body understands where this virulent fluid came from. Shakily I get to my feet, my body protesting after being in bondage for so long.

'You see how easy it is to obey?'

I nod, not in agreement but because there is nothing for me to say. I'm trembling, teetering on the edge of hysteria and orgasm. I am disgusting, an animal, a sick at heart whore turned on by drinking her own piss when commanded. The thought of what I have just done fills my mind, pushing everything else away, until there is just the image of me, naked and sharing my piss with another woman. I can feel it dribbling down my chin, warm wet rivulets that dapple my breasts with golden jewels.

If I touch myself I'm going to scream. If I touch myself I'm going to die in orgasm. I hold back, transfixed, unable to function without command. If Sister Catherine, holy bitch, tells me to get down on my knees and suck the piss from her cunt I'll do it gladly, losing myself in the very act of defilement. I want her to, need her to. Inside me, deep down in the blackest part of my soul, that's precisely what I long for.

'The lesson has only just begun,' I am warned. Still naked, I am led out of the room, trailing like a zombie behind Sarah and the holy Sister. Along silent corridors, cruising through an atmosphere of serenity and contemplation, I follow meekly and obediently.

When we pass one of the Sisters, anonymous in black, she barely registers my existence. My nakedness does nothing, it means nothing, it is my natural state to be unclothed and my feet unshod. From behind I cannot see the expression on Sarah's face. Does she share my feelings? Fuck it, the stupid bitch has slaked her thirst on my piss, that's got to count for something, *it has to.*

Into a large, spacious hall. Four sets of big square windows shed a weak, grey light that is the only illumination. It's enough to give a gloomy, tarnished atmosphere to the place. We are the only people here and the overwhelming impression I have is of emptiness, the high ceiling and the dimensions of the walls enclosing a space that is waiting to be filled.

'It will be time soon,' Sarah says, speaking to no one in particular.

'Have faith and be strong,' Sister Catherine advises, though there's nothing in her manner to suggest that this is anything but another instruction to be obeyed. To give support is not her way, to offer sympathy is a weakness she is never guilty of.

I remain silent. I'm not thinking about anything, not feeling anything but the embers of my desire dying down but ready to flare instantly. I don't want to know why Sarah should have faith and be strong. I don't care what it's going to be time for. It's easier not to think, anticipate or plan. If you think or plan then you'll always be disappointed, always, without exception.

Sarah begins to undress, shedding her robes, losing that black skin that shields her from pernicious thoughts and desires. In moments she is naked, pert little breasts peaked with tight round nipples. The bitch looks good, I'm sort of envious, with her girlie body she could make a mint, all it needs is the coy look and the little girl lost routine. Instead she stands awkwardly, trying hard to shield her pussy lips with her fingers, her eyes averted so they don't come into contact with mine. I figure it out then, when I realise it's my eyes she's avoiding and not bitch Sister's.

I turn her on, she is as excited by me as I am by her. I know she's still got the flavour of my piss in her mouth, and it turns her on, she's excited by our filthy act. What an angel, I'd bathe in her piss and share it in our mouths, I'd swim in her cunt juices, suck down her menstrual blood. My angel of filth, she's struggling with herself all for me. For me. Shit, there's no hope for the bitch.

'Hands and knees,' Sister Catherine snaps, clicking her fingers and pointing to the floor.

Sarah moves first, dropping as though felled. She kneels meekly just behind Sister Catherine, sitting like an obedient bitch at the heels of her mistress. I sit on the other side, so that there are two naked bitches flanking Sister, just the way it should be. The queen bitch has got to be happy, having two obedient little girl slaves at her heel. We are hers to do as she wishes with, whether it's for pain or pleasure or both. I sneak a look at Sarah, hoping that we can share a smile, hoping that down here, on the cold floor we can be equals. I don't have faith but so fuck, when you're on your knees does faith matter?

The door at the far side of the hall opens suddenly and a procession of identikit Sisters, black and white clones, faces blank, enter noiselessly like ghosts. Five of them, synchronised, floating across the hall towards us. A ceremony, I give up on Sarah, I know she's engrossed in what's happening while I'm engrossed in her. I long to touch her, to stroke those thighs that will tremble to my touch, to kiss those lips I have flavoured with my body.

The five Sisters glide to a halt and I see that they've been escorting a sixth, dressed as they are in black robes and white cowl. Only her face is pale, eyes barely open, jewels of sweat on her pallid skin. She walks jerkily; step, pause, step, and with every step her eyes flicker. The others form a circle around her, leaving one end open so that Sister Catherine can face directly.

'Forgive me, Sister, for I have sinned against all that is holy,' the girl whispers, her voice drifting in and out of focus. I swear she's about to topple over, she closes her eyes, waits, opens them slowly. 'I am penitent, Sister. Mortify my flesh so that I may be forgiven...'

Sister Catherine looks without emotion at the sick young woman before her, too weak to stand much longer, too ill to speak or see properly. It seems an age before bitch Sister nods her assent. 'We are merciful in this House,' she pronounces.

I can't believe what I've just heard. Fuck, did she really say 'merciful'? I want to laugh out loud, to sneer and spit in the face of this evil bitch who sees mercy as weakness. Sarah stands up, and I realise I have to follow. We stand, our nakedness ignored by the assembled Sisters, and take the few steps towards the penitent. I'm ready to catch her, sure she's about to collapse to the floor and smash her skull on the cold granite surface.

Sarah undoes the cowl and motions for me to remove the black robe. I unclip it at the back and together Sarah and I carefully draw it away. O shit. I stifle the gasp of horror that rises instinctively from my guts. The poor bitch is latticed with blood, a map of rivers drawn from her own body. She is wrapped tightly in steel wire, from her knees to her cunt and then again around her chest. Steel wire barbed viciously so that metal claws dig deep into her flesh. When she moves the wounds are opened and the blood pours. Every step is an agony she has endured. She is shaking, weak and delirious, blood pouring steadily from countless wounds.

I am pulled back, Sarah takes me by the arm and walks me back to Sister Catherine. On auto-pilot, I get down on hands and knees, submissively at heel. The penitent Sister takes another step forward, I catch the agony of pain that forces her eyes shut. She's close enough for me to see the steel barbs rip into her thighs and breasts. A walking crucifixion, she raises her face to heaven, offering herself. This is mercy, this is what they mean by mercy in this shit hole of a place.

Very slowly she gets down on hands and knees, the steel barbs pull harder and new wounds are ripped open. Cut and bleeding, I hear not a murmur of disgust, not a sigh of sympathy from anyone else in the room. And not from her, not from this poor sick, sick woman who's massacring herself for having sinned. Her breasts are veined with rivulets of blood, making her skin glossy, dripping like milk from her nipples. A parody of motherhood, I feel sick just watching her. How could they do this, how could they do this?

'There is only redemption through suffering,' Sister Catherine preaches in a voice so clear and powerful it fills the great hall. 'Do not seek to avoid suffering, rather it is better to accept it with an open, joyous heart. Pain is our Master, through pain we find wisdom and truth. Let us rejoice in the pain and suffering of our most penitent Sister. Do not feel false sympathy, you do her injury by wishing her pain away. Help her, help her in her weakness, to suffer all the more so that she may know the agonies and the ecstasies of pain. Open your hearts and take pride in her pain, accept the sweet joy with which this suffering is offered.'

One of the other Sisters steps forward. She's holding a book of scripture over the bloodied penitent and begins to read from it. '"This is a cause for great joy, even though you smart for a little while, if need be, under trails of many kinds. Even gold passes through the assayers fire, and more than perishable gold is faith which has stood the test. These trails come so that your faith may prove itself worthy of all praise, glory and honour when Jesus Christ is revealed."'

When she steps back another one takes her place, but instead of a book of scripture she wields a vicious looking whip. Her prim little fingers grip the short, padded handle, the long leather thongs that hang from the end of the handle are finished with thick, hard knots. The penitent is on hands and knees, her blood shot eyes fixed on the thonged whip.

'You're not going to...' I start to protest. A hard slap across the face throws me to the floor, the blood pouring from my lips. I look up at the queen bitch, but she doesn't deign to even look at me, even though the imprint of her fingers marks my face like a scar.

I lay there, face flat on the floor, letting the blood dribble from my mouth. There is nothing I can do but watch. The penitent is in profile, I can see the blood beginning to clot in places, in others it runs freely. Her breasts are caged by the barbed wire, cupped in place not with loving finery and pretty lace but cold steel and biting barbs. Her thighs are entwined by the wire, wrapped tightly so that the skin bulges against the constriction that tears at her.

The first blow of the whip comes down suddenly, the keening whistle turning into a hard snap of sound as the leather kisses the battered flesh of her back. The penitent moans as the pain tears through her, but she does not yield. Instead she looks at her tormentor with eyes that cry tears but carry no anger. The whip comes down again, harder, slicing into flesh already bloodied. I can see the red lines that the knots of leather slice into her, neatly parallel lines that run across her back. Harder, harder, each stroke seems to build on the power and intensity of the last. No let up, no mercy, there is a blur of motion as the whip swings back and forth, beating a rhythm on flesh.

The penitent weeps, tears running down her face, she writhes in pain and agony. At one point she collapses, falling forward so that the wire cuts deeper into her breasts. It makes no difference, the leather strands are already wet with her blood, each time the whip draws back it rains blood on the walls and onto the circle of nuns. When her blood splashes my face I close my eyes and it feels as though I am weeping as it trickles down my cheek. Sarah is transfixed, her eyes blazing intensely as she watches the ceremony proceed, her pale skin dappled with scarlet blood too.

When the penitent goes into spasm, rolling around the floor, screaming, wailing, her blood smearing over the stone, the whipping stops. She is awash with blood and spit and tears. Her eyes are wide, rolling in her head with a delirium that frightens me. The pain has to be unbearable, I cannot see how she can even move. I want her to black out, to lose consciousness so that something inside her can wipe it all away. Something inside me is coiled, wound down so tight I think I'm going to burst. I have experienced pain, pain so dreadful that I have gone under. Only now, seeing this, my own pain is ready to surface, the terror rising inside me like acid puke burning my throat.

Another Sister is already in place. She kneels beside the hysterical penitent, taking her carefully in her arms. Is it over? I long to see mercy, to witness one single act of kindness. Shit, I am a whore, an evil nasty little bitch who fucks for money but never have I felt so pure. The penitent stills, she is on her back, staring blankly into her comforter's eyes. She is off the planet, I can see the look in her eyes, the junked out look of ecstasy I have seen a million times before. Only it has always taken a fuck in the back of a car to get the junk or the money to buy the junk. Why is this bitch, bloody and beaten, so fucking high all of a sudden?

The cry of agony pulls me back to reality. The penitent is on her back, lying on the barbed wire devouring her flesh, while her legs have been forced open. Now a massive black dildo is being forced into the slick folds of her cunt. She is coming and screaming in agony at the same time. Her Sister, so merciful, is pushing the dildo in and out with a kind of vicious abandon. It seems to be splitting the girl in two, forcing her cunt open obscenely as she struggles to take it all. As wide as a fist, it goes in and out without rhythm, a violent motion is all that is required. Poor little bitch, she is being raped by her Sister, penetrated by an obscenely bloated dildo designed not for pleasure but for maximum pain.

She climaxes repeatedly, jabbering, speaking in tongues as the holy spirit is transmuted into an obscene pseudo-phallus sported by a holy Sister. And then she is turned partly onto her stomach, her buttocks are already marked red with the flogger. The Sister stands up, leaving the dildo in the penitent's bloody cunt, the tip protruding, glistening plastic wet with blood and cunt juice.

The third Sister from the circle takes her appointed place at the victim's side. She turns the penitent over completely, displaying the poor girl's backside, stripped red with the thonged whip. The dildo is pulled out of wet sex and forced violently into the penitent's arsehole. The scream of agony pierces everything, striking a note of fear deep within me. Why are they doing this? What the fuck do they hope to prove? I can feel the sick rising up within me, I'm going to puke my guts out.

With the same vicious strokes that she has been cunt raped, the penitent is anally penetrated using the dildo. I watch it disappearing between her round buttocks, pushing through her protesting arse to drive deep into her bowels. Her whole being shakes and heaves each time the dildo is forced in or out. She is writhing again, a hysterical creature driven beyond endurance. When she coils and pukes, spewing her guts all over the floor, all over herself, my guts churn in sympathy. Fuck. I watch her scream her climax as the dildo goes in again, hard and deep, burning deep into her rectum as she writhes like an epileptic.

She is released momentarily. She lies on her back, breasts rising and falling as she heaves for breath. Strung out, out of her tiny little mind, covered in blood and puke and come, it's hard to believe that she is still human. She is speaking in tongues, mumbling incoherently, writhing still, unable to control her own body.

I listen closely, the bitch is saying something, mumbling a prayer through cracked lips and dry mouth. 'O what pleasure, so real, so very real. Pain. Exhilarating. My body and I united. United at last. O, Master, thank you for this moment. This glimpse. O, Jesus. Let it hurt, every nerve screaming fire until I can take no more. Please, Lord, take me forever...'

A click of the fingers and Sarah crawls forward, looking to me to follow. I want to be sick too but somehow I push myself up from the floor and crawled into that circle of black robed Sisters. The ground is wet with sticky blood and stinking bilious puke, I crawl towards the young penitent, afraid that she's going to turn towards me and shut her eyes forever. That's what she wants, to be taken forever, to die for the good of her faith, for the glory of her belief. Stupid bitch, I want to beat her to her senses, to spit in her mouth, slap her face, to tell her: This is it, bitch! This is it, this is life! This is the best there is!

Sarah positions herself, sitting over the penitent girl's face. Without prompting the girl begins to suck and lick feverishly, using her mouth to explore Sarah's soaking pussy. The waves of pleasure that pass through Sarah are so obvious to see, the way she squirms and closes her eyes, the long exhaled sighs of ecstasy. The penitent sucks greedily, seeking every drop of moisture to slake her desire, pushing her face into Sarah's cunt as though she wants to lose herself in Sarah's body.

'O, Jesus, Jesus, thank you Lord,' Sarah cries, her pleasure merging with her faith as she climaxes violently over the penitent's mouth. Then she releases it, letting her piss flood into the girl's open, accepting mouth. I watch as the girl struggles to swallow it all, gulping it down greedily but unable to keep up with the flood. It pours from the sides of her mouth and down her face and chin, merging with the dried blood and the tears of joy which weeps ecstatically.

I hear the whimper of complaint as Sarah is moved away, the penitent wanting to carry on, seeking out the last droplets of piss with her tongue. Then it is my turn, I am motioned into place. I sit back, looking down at the bruised and battered body as I feel the girl's lips beginning to suck the wetness from my cunt. And I am wet, cunt soaked through with a desire that makes me sick to my stomach. Why do I have to be so wet? Why am I so fucking turned on by this sick, disgusting ceremony? I have no faith, no belief, all I have is this body and yet it betrays me.

Her tongue is making me moan, she knows how to suck, the bitch. In her delirium she is making me come within seconds. She laps at my clit, teasing it so that I might flood her mouth with my juice. She wants it, and she wants my piss too. Anything, she is ready for anything. How much fucking pain does she have to take, so much suffering just so that she can suck cunt? Why? Why? Why?

And then, suddenly I am pushed further forward and her tongue is lapping at my arsehole. She pushes her tongue into me and I climax. I hadn't expected that, the pleasure is strange, so intense that I feel it in my cunt and on my nipples. She is sucking my arsehole, licking it as though it's the most precious thing in the world. Deeper, deeper, she touches and strokes, her tongue expertly giving me pleasure in my anal hole.

'Now, empty your bowels,' Sister Catherine orders, standing in front of me, an expression of stern pleasure lighting up her face.

'No!' I scream, trying to pull myself away. The penitent bitch is trying to suck out the shit from inside me. Her tongue is seeking it out, going into me in the hope that she might swallow whatever filth she finds inside my shit hole.

I scramble away as I puke, the fire roaring through my throat as I empty myself on the floor. There are murmurs of complaint and then there is silence. I turn and see that Sarah is over the girl's mouth again, only this time it's her arsehole being tongued. With a horror that makes me puke again, I see her pushing out her soft brown waste into the grateful mouth of her penitent Sister.

SEVEN

I puke again when I'm pushed into the shower, the dry retching of my throat spewing forth only foul tasting yellow bile. It splashes on the cold tiled floor and I fall next to it, weeping like a child. My mind in turmoil, I want to weep and scream, to escape forever this nightmare of a life. My hair is matted, sticking to my face, my body shivering from cold and fear.

'What she would not give willingly, you'll take by force,' Sister Catherine orders two of her minions. She glares at me for a moment longer and then turns to leave, followed by Sarah, who seems as lost as I am.

'You make me sick!' I scream hoarsely, anger and rage fighting through the tears. I want to fight them, these evil witches parading as holy women. Sisters of degradation, defilement and despair, I want to destroy them all.

My tormentors, two of the five in the penitent's ceremonial circle, stand over me. I can't tell what they're thinking, there's nothing in their expressions that I can make out. I am lost, irretrievable, forever.

One of them unravels a length of hose, a long line attached to one of the taps on the wall. I've been pushed into the communal shower, a dark room with tiled floor and walls, drains along the ground and shower heads hanging overhead. A sparse affair, I am not even to enjoy that, sitting naked on the floor the tap is turned slowly until a trickle of water leaks like piss from the end of the hose.

'Leave me alone, you fucking slags, you fucking shit eating bitches...' I wail as they advance on me. I'm too tired to stand and fight, I barely have enough energy to crawl backwards in a feeble effort to get away from them. My knees are scuffed against the stone tiles and my arms shake as I crawl towards the furthest corner of the room.

I am seized by the waist just as my arms give way. I fall forwards, my breasts crushed against the tiles and my face flat on the ground. The world is spinning around me, turning violently this way and that as I fight to retain control. There is nothing left for me to puke, I am empty but still I retch and heave painfully. Powerful hands hold me in place, my backside sticking up, knees pulled apart. The cold water splashes between my thighs, making me shiver even more. I'm going to be hosed down, denied the dignity of a proper shower, washed like a dirty and disobedient animal.

The water is squirted over my thighs and lower back, an icy jet that strokes me intimately. Then, as I'm held down, the tube is pushed against my anal-hole. I try to resist, try to squeeze my buttocks together. I'm slapped hard, repeatedly, cold hands spanking me swiftly until the pain is too much. My strength spanked away, the fire burning on my arse cheeks turning to fire in my pussy as well. The cold water does nothing to soothe the pain away and then the hose is pushed hard into my anal hole.

'You fucking bitches... You dirty whores...' I scream and weep. The icy water fills my guts, freezing me from the inside. In seconds my belly is distended, filled with ice cold water that makes my teeth shiver. I look like a pregnant bitch, a sow on hands and knees with bulging belly. The tube is pushed in further, held in place by my silent tormentors.

'Empty yourself!' I'm ordered, as though I have a choice. The hose is pulled out quickly and I can't control myself. The filth is expelled violently from my arse, squirting out across the floor and then down my thighs. If I had any more to puke it would join the stinking mess around me.

I sit there, surrounded by my own bodily wastes, sitting in the human slurry of my shit. Tears pour down my face as I weep like a child. Powerless. They won't even let me shit or piss when I want to, that would be too much of an honour for a whore like me. What do I expect? Do I really imagine that my life is worth any more than this? Fucking stupid bitch, who do I think I am?

The hose is turned on me, at full blast, soaking my face and body, my hair and limbs. Washed down like an animal, scrubbed clean because I can't do it myself. The jets of water squirt down, pushing my shit down the drains and with it any dignity I once had. I am turned over and washed, rough hands brushing against my nipples, my cunt, my arse. They pull me to my feet and let the water run down my back and legs, slapping my thighs and calves when I don't move the way they want me to.

Finally it is over, and dripping water I am hauled roughly out of the shower and into the changing room next door. I reach blindly for a towel but am slapped again, hard smacks of the hand turning my breasts pink and nipples red. How dare I imagine that I can dry myself? I am rubbed down in silence, the water patted away quickly, the towel roughly wiping against my body. An animal, helpless, they are there to clean me because I am not human enough to do it myself. I lack the faith. If only I too could eat shit in the name of the Lord, if only I could suffer with joy in my heart, if only.

Then I am allowed food. On hands and knees of course, eating from a bowl like a good little bitch. Any attempt to use my hands mean more slaps, or a kick in the rump, or a sharp tugging at my hair. Little bitch has got to eat like a little bitch. I obey, too tired and disoriented to do anything else but comply. What right do I have to refuse? I deserve it, I deserve everything, always.

◆

'You disappoint me,' Sister Catherine remarks flatly, regarding me with grey eyes that eat like acid. She looks so good, a strict vision in black and white, smooth skin and a sensuous mouth. She is sitting behind her desk, looking down at me, curled up and shivering at her side.

I'm exhausted, without energy or emotion, numbed by pain and shock. I look at her and know that there's no emotion in my eyes either, I have been drained of feeling just as I have been drained of shit and piss. I am a shell of a person, a body reduced to component parts that move mechanically.

'There is much that you can learn from us,' she continues, her eyes still fixed on me, as though she's expecting a response. 'And there's much that some of the Sisters can learn from you, also.'

No response, I stare back at her without seeing or thinking. I'm naked at her feet, chin resting on my knees, arms wrapped tightly to keep myself warm. Let me curl up, let me become foetal not just faecal, let me retreat. It's better not thinking, not doing, not being. I don't want life, I just want to exist.

'You realise I have to punish you for your outburst earlier,' she tells me, though her voice lacks the triumphalism I would have adopted in her place. I don't even shrug, I expected nothing less than punishment, it feels like my whole life revolves around it. Life isn't a reward, it's a punishment which we suffer because there's nothing else, because we have no choice.

Sarah joins us, she glides into the room, graceful as an angel, dressed in the uniform of her vocation. She glances at me, a swift look in my direction, and then she faces Our Sister. In that one moment I can't tell what went through her mind, did she feel sympathy or pity for me? I fight to rid my mind of the image of Sarah, beautiful and angelic, shitting into the penitent's mouth. But I can't do it, I can't shut it out, it'll be with me always, always.

'To beat you would not be punishment enough,' Sister Catherine continues, addressing me and ignoring Sarah completely. 'I suspect that you would find comfort in the pain,' she adds with a hint of a smile. 'Your punishment has to go beyond mere physical pain, I want it to reach deeper, I want to touch you in ways you do not even suspect exist.'

I listen in silence, cold dread growing as she speaks. She is a whore, I know it, and she frightens me because she understands me completely. I'm afraid because she doesn't lie, there is no doubt that her dead eyes have seen more than I will ever experience. There is nothing that I can imagine that Sister Whore has not experienced, my worst nightmares are sweet dreams in her reality.

She turns her attention to Sarah. 'What is suffering?' she demands.

'To suffer is holy, in suffering we are in mind of the Lord,' Sarah replies promptly and with feeling.

'And unearned suffering?'

'I remember the first letter of Peter: "Servants, be subject to your masters with all due submission, not only when they are good and gentle, but even when they are perverse. For it is a fine thing if a man endure the pain of undeserved suffering because the Lord is in his thoughts..."'

Sister Catherine smiles. "'What glory is there in fortitude when you have done wrong and are beaten for it? But when you have done well and suffer for it, your fortitude is a fine thing in the eyes of the Lord.'" she says, taking up the quote. 'You have pleased me today, you have performed your duties with a joy that reflects well on your spiritual progress.'

Sarah blushes, a shy smile forming on her pretty lips. 'You stupid bitch,' I whisper under my breath, sickened by her attitude of complete submission, an attitude that is alien to me but central to her. That's it, that's why I can never have faith, I cannot submit.

'Sarah, undress,' Our Sister commands suddenly. 'This is your punishment,' she tells me, 'you are to beat her with the whip until the blood flows from her back.'

I look at her for a moment before speaking. 'Get fucked,' I say quietly, 'you can play your own sick games from now on.'

'Do you think that I am offended by the vulgarities you dare to utter?' she asks, raising her eye brows questioningly. 'Or do you imagine that you will provoke me to use the whip on your back?'

'I don't care, you do what you fucking want,' I shrug, wrapping my arms tighter around my knees. She could beat me if she wanted to, but no matter how much pain I would endure I would still be the winner, it would not be the submission she demands.

'You like Sarah,' she points out, 'if I asked you to beat another of the Sisters would you comply? No? If you were asked to beat the flesh from my back?'

'You'd fucking enjoy it, because you're a sick, evil bitch faking religion to get your kicks,' I tell her, beginning to regain the spirit that is mine.

'You find comfort in your own words,' Sister Catherine guesses, 'but your words are empty. You seek strength where there is none. Without faith your words are meaningless.'

'This is boring, you're not convincing me, you're just a cheap fucking whore the same as me. How'd you get here? You belong on the streets sucking cock for the night and selling your arsehole to any man with the money...'

'Stop that! Stop it!' Sarah snaps, turning on me with fire in her eyes. She is angry, real passion in her voice, really shocked by what I'm saying. Fuck it, what is wrong with the girl? Bitch Sister is unmoved by my taunts, but her little slave girl, who has every reason to hate Sister, is angered. I fall silent, avoiding Sarah's anger because I am strangely in awe of it.

'Sarah, do you have sins to expiate?' Sister asks, sitting back in her seat confidently.

'Yes, Sister, there are sins in my heart.'

I sneer dismissively. 'What fucking sins have you committed? Apart from the sin of terminal fucking stupidity?'

'If you are not beaten now, for sins unearned, then tomorrow you will take part in the circle of penance.'

'What?' I demand angrily. 'What do you mean?'

Sarah looks at me mournfully. 'If you do not beat me now, as Our Sister commands you to,' she explains patiently, 'then tomorrow I will take part in the ceremony you witnessed today.'

I feel the world falling away from me again. It's just too sick to be true. 'They're going to shit in your mouth? You're going to be wrapped in barbed wire and beaten?' Sarah nods gravely. 'Say no!' I cry. 'Just say no, you don't have to do it, you've got a choice,' I insist hoping against hope that she'll listen. It's a waste of time, she is sorrowful but not because of what's going to happen but because I am arguing against Sister's edicts. She wants it, she wants to be beaten and humiliated, she wanted to be defiled and debased. She wants it, wants it, wants it.

'Tomorrow you will defile her mouth,' Sister Catherine adds, smiling cruelly. 'If you again refuse then Sarah will suffer the same ceremony again and again until you obey.'

I have a vision of Sarah feasting on shit and suffering everyday. Day after day of agony until I squat over her and empty myself into her mouth. I vividly imagine her tongue cleaning my soiled anus, seeking out every morsel of filth in order to expiate crimes she has not even committed. Could hell be this perverse, this sick? Religion has slaughtered millions on the battle field, and yet there are willing victims ready to lose themselves totally to its primal ecstasies.

'Why are you so evil?' I ask, defeated by their purity of faith.

'Without faith, without love for our creator, you do not even understand the nature of good and evil,' comes the stark reply. 'Is it goodness that drives you to sell your body for money? Is it evil that we give our bodies to suffering so that we are cleansed in the sight of the Lord?'

'I'm not going to shit in your mouth,' I promise Sarah. 'I'd rather whip the skin off your bones than do that.'

'And why is the one better than the other?' Sister Catherine demands, laughing because I make such an irrational choice.

'How the fuck should I know?' I answer, rising unsteadily to my feet. Sarah is already undressing, exposing the smooth skin of her back. The whip is there on the desk, waiting for me to wield it with a viciousness that is going to draw blood.

'Hurt her,' Our Sister instructs coldly.

I pick up the whip, strands of leather tightly wound to create one long lash of black braid. This is a whip designed to hurt, lovingly crafted to cut into flesh and draw blood and screams at the same time. It frightens me, I become aware suddenly that I have it in my power to cause damage, lasting physical damage.

'Make her scream,' Sister Catherine insists, her voice as steely as her grey eyes. Sitting back in her throne, she is revelling in her power, certain that both Sarah and I will perform to instruction.

When I turn round Sarah is in place, naked and facing the wall. She is beautiful, stretched out, arms on the wall, legs parted, bent slightly at the waist. A child, she can't be older than me, why is she doing this? I want to weep for her, my life is shit but she chose to travel this sick path and I didn't. Her pussy is almost bare, the blonde fringe of hair that covers her cunt is almost invisible. She has a body I could worship, I'd get down on my knees and lick her pussy lovingly. What pleasures we could share, and she'd respond, I know she would.

'Be strong,' Sarah says, quietly. I can see the desire in her eyes, burning fervently. The little bitch wants to suffer, she longs for the torment that will turn pain into pleasure, that will drive her from this reality into blissed out ecstasy.

I raise the whip, letting it uncoil completely. I've never used a whip like this before, the tail is too long for me to have complete control. I snap it once, it thunders in the room and I hear Sarah moan softly. I walk across to her, sick at heart because I know what I'll find. When I push my fingers into her pussy she's wet, soaked by the sexual desire that she does not acknowledge. I fuck her hard with my fingers, penetrating brutally, making her moan deliriously. The bitch, she's fucking turned on by the idea of being beaten, turned on by the pain that's going to slice through her.

'Hurt her!' Sister Catherine hisses through clenched teeth. She doesn't want me to finger fuck little Sister, she wants me to beat her till the blood spurts.

I scream as my fury is vented. The whip whistles through the air, slicing the atmosphere, cleaving it in two as it travels so fast and furious. It cuts, snapping hard into skin that opens like a flower. The blood pours, scarlet against flawless white skin. Bitch! Again. I beat her with all my strength, arm coming down and the tip of leather travelling a graceful arc. She screams, voice ripping through her mouth like projectile vomit. It hurts, bitch, it hurts. I strike again, without mercy, ripping her back open, letting the blood pour. O, you stupid bitch, why this? Why this? Again, harder, sweat pours from my body as the blood pours from hers. She's still standing, pressed against the wall, arms outstretched all the better to hurt her. Why doesn't she fall, why doesn't she let herself fall to the floor like an abject animal?

I'm the one weeping, crying, sobbing like a child. I can't go on, I can't hurt her any more. I drop the whip and rush to her, wanting to hold her in my arms. I want to kiss away the blood, to run my tongue along the grooves I've cut into her. She is trembling, eyes wide with pain and anguish. 'Let me kiss you,' I whisper urgently, concern filling my voice. Through my tears I seek hers.

'Beat me!' she whispers urgently, the need so clear and strong. 'Beat me more.'

I step away, unable to comprehend the madness I see before me. Her back is scarred and bleeding, but it's not enough for her. I drop to my knees and crawl towards her again. I can't give up on her, I have to reach her, have to save her from herself.

Pan Panziarka

She doesn't understand that it can be different.

I crawl to her and begin to use my mouth and tongue on her backside. I lick her anal hole with my tongue, I trace the anal cleft until I reach her sex. She's so wet and I begin to suck the goodness from her cunt, I press deeper and she bends lower. Her sighs of pleasure spur me on, the pain must be unbearable but I want to show her the other way. She orgasms with a moan of complaint, as though she doesn't want it. I don't stop, my hands part her arse-cheeks and I kiss her rosy back hole again, pressing my tongue sensuously against it.

The snap of leather and her scream coincide. I half turn and see Sister Catherine holding the whip. I can't stop, I can't. Sarah moans as I return to her arsehole, my fingers caressing her clit so that she's being pleasured front and rear. Only this time her moans of pleasure are intersected by the crack of the whip and her piercing screams which follow.

Sarah is suffering, but she suffers beautifully.

♦

Eyes only half open, head drooping wearily, I long for sleep to rid me of this sick reality. Let me find the darkness that is release, I'll accept it gladly, gratefully. I don't want this, not any of it. Why me? What have I done to deserve this? I'm an obscene little bitch, selling my snatch for money, selling my body night after night but somehow that is clean compared to this. Sex is honest, it might be dirty and disgusting but somehow it's honest. Sucking cock is honest, being fucked is honest, even being beaten for kicks is honest. Where's the honesty in suffering for religion? Where's the honesty in eating shit for your faith, in drinking piss or being beaten or sucked or fucked for the good of the Lord?

Shit, I don't care any more. I'm too tired. Hands cuffed behind my back, sitting on my arse by the big desk in Sister Catherine's room. Jesus loves me, my saviour with the suffering in his eyes looks down on me. The bastard, I can see it in his eyes, under that loin cloth he's sporting a hard on that would shame a donkey. How many times did he come while they were nailing him to that cross? How much spunk dribbled down those emaciated thighs, mingling with blood and water in his ecstasy of crucifixion? He stares at me now, from the portrait on the wall and his secret is revealed, the hidden knowledge open to my tired eyes.

'Why do you persist?' Our Sister asks, crossing the room to take her imperious place behind the desk. She seems refreshed, her brisk manner reflected in the clarity of her voice.

'How the fuck do I know?' I reply, irritated by her attitude. And it's true, how the fuck should I know?

'You take so much pleasure in your torments,' she continues, ignoring my question, 'you should be happy helping me here. The road should be easy for you, there is much that is familiar to you already.'

'I don't know what you mean,' I murmur, looking at her with eyes that can barely open.

'No matter how much you suffer you are not redeemed, your spirit remains untouched by all that happens to you. When you are beaten the pain turns to pleasure, but that pleasure is purely physical there is no spiritual dimension to it. Do you see? Where Sister Sarah finds transcendence and enlightenment you find nothing but humiliation, and in that process you steal your pleasure.'

'And?' I ask, waiting for the punch line.

'You can help me,' she tells me, allowing herself a rare smile.

Pan Panziarka

We're alone, and for the first time I realise she's trying to tell me something that I can understand and use. 'How?' I ask. 'How can I help you?'

'Be merciless in your pleasures,' she counsels. 'Seek total gratification, without limit, without pity and in the process help others find the spiritual truths that they seek.'

I look at her for a moment, I can barely focus. 'You mean I can do what I like, I can fuck, hurt, humiliate, without any limits, just so long as I pretend I'm doing it for God?'

'Faith needs to be tested,' she explains. 'Our Lord sends sickness to destroy babies, hunger to wipe out thousands, war to waste the innocent. He takes mothers from children, wives from their husbands. Without mercy, without pity, he causes pain and suffering in untold measure. He does not want us to forget, he wants us to love him with fear in our hearts. The torments that we suffer in this house are but nothing, such petty tests when the world is tested always.'

'Do you believe that shit?' I hear myself ask. My eyes are closed and the darkness is rushing to take me.

I think I can hear her voice, but it's so very distant. '*It means nothing. All is vanity. When life is goodness, when the world is sweetness, then remind yourself: It means nothing*'.

EIGHT

It means nothing. I wake up and it's there, in my head, my mantra, my credo, alpha and omega, the beginning and the end. There is no hope. I *know*, I can feel it, physically, there in the pit of my stomach. The universe doesn't care. There is no point, no meaning, nothing. Where does that lead me? Accept the truth. It means nothing. No one cares. History is shit. Life is shit. There is no hope and no future. Who gives a fuck? Abandon hope, light is always temporary, darkness is eternal. Understand that and rejoice in it.

I'm naked, sitting on the edge of my bed after sleeping on the floor all night with my hands cuffed behind my back. At my feet there's a sweet young innocent, a pretty little Sister wide eyed and innocent. She has brought my robes, as black as hers only I know that there's light inside her and nothing inside me. On her knees and nervous, she doesn't know what to do or say.

'Do you know why I'm here?' I ask her, the first words I've spoken to her since she escorted me to this cell and presented me with the vestments of my newly discovered vocation.

'Yes, Sister,' she replies, her sweet voice trembling with emotion, 'you are to help guide us on the holy path.'

I nod. It's a fucking rocky path this one, strewn with sorrows and agonies which have to be suffered by the repentant sinner. 'Do you know your Scripture?' I ask her knowingly. I don't, but who cares? I can sound like one of them: if it hurts then it's good, if it doesn't hurt then it will soon.

'Yes, Sister, I study diligently,' she assures me like an eager young school girl.

I nod again. 'Which is best, suffering that is earned or unearned?' I ask, trying to remember the words that Sarah, my dear Sister in the service of the Lord, quoted previously.

'Unjust suffering is redemptive,' is the reply, which sounds right. Dying of cancer is better than dying of old age, right? Being eviscerated as a civilian in time of war is better than dying in your bed in time of peace, right? Starving to death is better than dying of obesity. Death is better than life. Darkness is holier than the light.

I look at her, look at her big brown eyes full of sadness. I stand up, pressing my cunt against her face. I reach down, part her lips with my fingers, push my pussy lips to her mouth. I'm wet, her tongue touches the wetness in my sex, makes me quiver with excitement. And then I piss. Into her mouth. Waves of it, waves of warm, yellow piss. She drinks it, choking to keep up, careful not to spill a drop, crying silently as the tears fall from her eyes tightly shut.

Doing holy work. This is my vocation now, this is where I have been led. I ought to say a prayer now, thank the Lord for his unbounded generosity.

'Thank you, Sister,' she whispers, wiping her mouth with the back of her hand. She's pale and I can see she's desperately trying not to puke, trying to hold in that acrid acid that I pissed for her. All day she'll have that inside her, the taste flavouring everything she eats or drinks. She thanks me, the stupid bitch, for being Sisterly enough to piss in her sweet little mouth.

'Where do I go once I'm dressed?' I ask, unfolding the heavy cotton uniform she's brought for me to wear.

'Sister Catherine is waiting for you.'

'Will you tell her what I've done?' I ask, unable to suppress my smile.

She nods gravely. 'I must report everything that has occurred between us,' she tells me. 'Just as I will mention it at confession.'

'What penance will you get for it?' I ask, as though she's confessing to mildly sinful thoughts or a bout of petty shop lifting.

She looks away from me. 'I confess I felt revulsion, the sin of pride touched my heart and... I did not understand why... You're not even a novice Sister...'

'You mean you don't know why you have to suck piss from a dirty cunt like mine?' I laugh, enjoying the redness of her face as she blushes with pure unadulterated shame.

'I am sorry, Sister,' she murmurs humbly. The stupid bitch is apologetic, for real. Now I can see why Sister Catherine wants me, how much more humiliating it is for these fucking idiots to be demeaned by a cheap whore like me. Eating my shit must be the ultimate penance, a force 10 on the Richter scale of religious debasement.

I follow her back to Sister Catherine's office, only this time I look like one of them, clad in black, body hidden, walking like a ghost through silent corridors. It feels strange, as though by donning this garb of piety I too have become pious and holy. As I glide behind my anonymous and innocent young Sister, I can see myself, blending into the ways of this House, transformed by the very act of wearing the uniform. Is this what happens? I can see it, accepting the veil and renouncing self, adopting the pose that the uniform requires.

Sister Catherine is waiting for us, seated regally behind her desk, there's no avoiding the look of impatience in her eyes. She's been waiting, bitch Sister, to see if I'm with her or not. And if I'm not? She'll make me pay, I know that for certain. Every ounce of evil will be brought to bear, she'll make me suffer all the ways there are to suffer. My nightmares of electrocution, those vague vestiges of memory that haunt me, will be nothing beside the torments she has ready for me. The whore hates me with an emotionless intensity that she nurses like a rare and exotic bloom. She hates me, but it's the hatred a sister has for a sister, the hatred a daughter has for her mother. And that's what we are, blood relations, whores under the skin and down to the bone.

'Well?' she demands, not of me but of my naive young escort, who shrinks visibly in the presence of Our Sister. They dread her, fear her as much as they fear the Lord Himself, all of them. Except me. I'm scared of her too, but my fear's less heavenly than theirs. I don't give a fuck about eternal damnation in the next world, all I care about is damnation in this one.

The smile on Sister Catherine's tells me I've performed well. My virtuous young victim is red in the face, unable to find the words to answer. 'She sinned,' I tell Our Sister, smiling.

'How did she sin?'

'I tested her, I emptied my bladder into her mouth and she felt nothing but revulsion,' I report earnestly, trying to adopt the same kind of dispassionate tone that bitch Sister has.

'Is this true?'

A shameful nod of the head and a steady flow of tears are the only response. Poor little bitch can't lie, the truth is all that matters and that's buried deep in her heart. She makes me angry, suddenly, for being so fucking pathetic. What does she expect? Stupid bitch! She wants to be punished, she's inviting it, begging for it like a dirty slut.

'Then you must be punished,' is the inevitable conclusion. 'When your body is defiled do not turn away,' Sister Catherine instructs nobly, 'rather accept it with joyous heart. You are nothing and it is false pride to cling to self. If the Lord chooses to test your love for Him, then do not feel revulsion, feel glad. Revulsion comes from you, from you and not from your love of His goodness.'

'Yes, Sister,' the girl sobs, tears streaming down her face. She looks so young, a child and yet she speaks without hope.

'Punish her,' Sister Catherine tells me, her eyes sparkling wickedly.

How? Does she want me to shit in the girl's mouth? Or beat her with a whip? The girl is mine, completely at my mercy. 'Undress,' I order, without knowing exactly what I want. I watch, enjoying the sense of power. The pretty face is matched by a pretty body, smooth skin, long legs, large breasts with big brown nipples and dark hair between the thighs.

'Take your sandals off,' I suggest, pointing to the girl's leather sandals. She bends down meekly, her long black hair covering her face and shoulders as she loosens the straps that bind up her ankles. Roman sandals, flat leather sole and tight leather straps, perfect for what I have in mind. I feel angry, violent.

I throw one of the sandals to the floor and then carefully wrap the straps of the other one around my wrist. Holding the sole firmly at the heel I slap the hard leather surface into my palm, the sound echoes round the room and the heat burns my hand. I'm glad it fucking hurts.

'Come here!' I snap, hissing through gritted teeth. She approaches hesitantly, eyes darting towards Sister Catherine in the vain hope of a reprieve. 'You must accept your punishments in the way they are intended,' I tell her. 'These things are meant to test you, we perform these acts because we love you. See? We hurt you for your own good.'

I guess that sounds like a load of shit because Our Sister intervenes. 'Renounce flesh, renounce pride, renounce yourself,' she intones sombrely. 'We mortify the flesh to be reminded of our Lord and in that suffering we find Him and our love for Him. Suffering is holy my child, it feeds the spirit and cleanses the flesh.'

That still sounds like shit to me, but it's holy shit so it must be alright. At least our little victim accepts it as a great truth, you can see it in her eyes. She wants to lose herself, she wants to destroy herself completely for the glory of the Lord. I pull her towards me, digging my nails into her shoulder. She winces but makes no complaint, not even a murmur of protest, dumb insolence is a language she's never mastered. She stands before me, head bowed but her body straight, tensed up. I run my fingers over her breasts, tracing the contours of her body and enjoying the horror that I know she's experiencing. Being touched like an animal, toyed with casually. Is she turned on, bitch? Is she?

I pinch her nipples hard and they double in size, reddish brown and erect. She's the sort of bitch that can come from having her tits played with, I can see that. Fuck, I'd give anything to pimp her, to put her on a street corner and sell her to the lowest of the low. I'd give her away just to see the shame in her eyes, I'd slap her in public and have her chasing me devotedly, that's the sort of whore she'd make.

'Next time!' I hiss, bringing the leather sandal down on her chest with an explosion of sound and a cry of agony from her lips. 'Next time you'll thank me!'

I hit her again, on the other side, smacking with all my might so that her skin is blood red and her nipples scarlet. It hurts all right, I can feel the pain radiating through the room. Again, harder. She buckles, stumbles momentarily but straightens up. She cries, lovely tears trickling down her sweet innocent face. I feel pity and so strike again, harder and harder until she screams and falls to her knees. She's trembling, her chest patterned with thick red stripes. I wind her long hair in my hand and pull it tight, making her cry out again.

'Next time you'll thank me!' I hiss, pulling her to her feet. She opens her mouth to speak and I spit in it, shooting a mouthful of spit like a projectile into her mouth. She swallows, with eyes closed and joy in her heart.

When I let go she falls on the floor crying. Without prompting she crawls forward, barely able to control herself and touches her lips to my feet. Tears rain down on my toes but I kick her away. No mercy, bitch. This is what she wants, this is the help she needs to find her way in the world. Be grateful that I'm here, to help you in your hour of need, stupid cunt that you are.

'Excellent,' Sister Catherine tells me when we're alone.

'That cunt needed it,' I tell her, breathing hard. I'm all psyched up, adrenaline pumping so that my heart's fit to go nova. If they drag the bitch back in I'd kill her, I'd dig my nails so deep into her skin I'd scrape bone. I hate her with a passion that makes me grit my teeth and spit blood.

'Please, no profanity,' I'm told sternly. 'There is still much for you to learn. Scripture study is important, do not imagine that it isn't...'

Pan Panziarka

I don't give a fuck about Scripture. 'How far can you go?' I ask, interrupting the boring stuff. 'How extreme does it get here?'

'The body has an almost infinite capacity for suffering,' the voice of experience tells me. 'Do not forget that in the rapture of communion with the Lord, the body ceases to matter, the thresholds of pain no longer apply.'

'Do you burn? Brand? Cut? Maim?' I demand, visions of violent excess burning feverishly in my warped imagination.

'There are no limits,' Our Sister tells me, her voice lowered as if to emphasise the full importance of what she's just said. No limits. None.

'What about... What about death?' I ask, quietly, hardly daring to breathe.

Bitch Sister doesn't blink. 'To die a martyr's death is beautiful,' she pronounces wistfully. 'Think of it, to lose the body, the spirit to ascend... To die is beautiful, to die for the Lord is the ultimate proof of devotion and love.'

What can I say? The evil bitch is moved almost to tears just thinking of the beauty of death. Fuck it, I always imagined that love is about life, but then a stupid bitch like me knows no better. That's why I need to study, the Scriptures most hold the key. Once I've studied, once I can quote the words as if they're truly mine, when I can speak with a voice that isn't my own, then I'll understand how you can turn love into death and devotion into denial.

'Are you alarmed?' Sister Catherine asks, her cold eyes catching the shock that I realise is on my face. I should know better, she's here because she's a perceptive bitch, she notices everything and understands it all.

I shrug. 'Yeah,' I mumble, 'I'm sort of shocked. I mean you've just told me that people die here, isn't that what you mean? People are killed to prove their devotion to God. Sacrifices, right? Human sacrifices.'

She laughs. 'I shouldn't be surprised,' she tells me indulgently. 'Why are so many of you girls so sentimental? Do you imagine that walking the streets and selling your body for money is not a sacrifice? Perhaps you imagine that working for a pittance is better, or that slaving for a husband is a more noble calling? I would have thought that you'd be inured to this sentimental nonsense. Life is sacrifice, it cannot be any other way.'

'But... But to die like that...'

'They die with fire in their eyes, lost in the most rapturous ecstasies of the soul. Ask these noble Sisters, do you think that any one of them would turn back? They have only to glimpse the ecstasies of death to know that it is their ultimate destination.'

'You're right,' I sigh, shaking off the sense of horror that's creeping up on me, 'I've got a lot to learn.'

She smiles approvingly. 'I know that you'll be an able student. Your program begins today. The rules of our House are most strict, as you are already aware. You will return to your room to study, a text has been selected for you, and you will remain there until called,' her voice becomes colder as she outlines the rules. 'On no account are you to leave your room, nor are you to speak with anyone. Food and water will be brought to you, but do not attempt to speak or to test the Sister who brings it you. A special ceremony takes place this evening, you will witness but not take part.'

'What sort of ceremony?'

Pan Panziarka

'Do not be impatient,' she tells me mysteriously. 'Now, retire to your room. Do not make the mistake of ignoring the text you are to study. Your knowledge will be tested, and should you not have progressed sufficiently well then punishment will be swift and painful.'

She means it, and we both know it. There's no way I want to get a glimpse of the ecstasies she talks about, I just don't want to have to take that much pain.

♦

The chapel is down in the guts of the building, in the bowels way down. I follow down narrow stairs, aware that as we descend the air is becoming warm and humid. My escort is the brown eyed Sister from the morning, her eyes barely meet my own, she's still embarrassed about sucking the piss from my cunt. Or else she doesn't know I'm under orders not to talk or do anything to her. I'd like to. I'd like to have her kneel down, I'd make the pretty little slut suck my pussy until I come in her mouth, and then I'd make her suck my arsehole until I climax again. I'd pull her hair and slap her around, make her my slut and tell her she's doing it for her faith.

The rough hewn steps lead to a corridor that looks as if it's cut from bare rock. Shit, it looks so old I'd swear it's older than the rest of the building. I can see how that would be, building on some dark cavern, erecting this house of pain on a network of medieval chambers. Blood has been shed here in the past, it's seeped into the foundations and pervades the cloistered air.

The chamber is at the end of the corridor, and as we approach I can hear the murmur of voices and the chant of prayer. It's dark down here, and when the door opens I can hardly see a thing. The smell of incense fills the air, mingling in some strange way with the murmured prayers that echo round the large round room. The only light is from the flickering candles that burn everywhere, the light dancing in the shadows and the smell of burning wax becoming one with the smell of incense. The atmosphere's intense, I've never seen so many Sisters gathered together before, there must be at least twenty of them.

It's hard to tell them apart. It's never struck me before how medieval they all look, long black gown, kirtle that wraps the head and neck exposing a disembodied face, sandals that scrape along the floor. In this darkness, in this pit, time means nothing, it has neither advanced nor retreated. But it's not the Sisters that I'm interested in, it's the crucifix in the centre that draws my attention. Made from thick beams of dark wood, the cross is on its side, as though it's toppled over. The central object of devotion, a circle of candles burns all around it, a circle of fire that throws shadows in all directions.

Sister Catherine is leading the prayer, her voice low and deep, echoing around the room as her words are taken up by her fellow Sisters. I take my place, standing in the circle, intoxicated by the dense atmosphere. When I breathe my lungs are filled with incense and it makes my head spin. Shit, I swear you can get high on this stuff.

The prayer stops suddenly and Our Sister breaks the circle. She strides forward and then turns to face us, in the darkness it's hard to see her face but her eyes are wild. She raises her hands, petitioning the Lord, and begins to speak in a loud, clear voice.

'Witness this cross, alone, neglected, of no value without its crucified. Do not forget that this cross is your cross. This is the cross we bear each day, the hidden cross, the cross of our hearts, the cross of our spirit. This is the cross that awaits its crucified. This is the cross that awaits completion and splendour. The Gospels remind us: "And whosoever shall exalt himself shall be abased; and he that shall humble himself shall be exalted". Bring forth the sinner...'

The circle parts and two Sisters escort a third figure, unclothed apart from a cloth around the waist. I can't see properly, my eyes are stinging and filled with tears. Fuck! It's a man, a near naked man. He's weak, body bathed in a glossy layer of sweat, hardly able to stand. I must have missed the first part of the ceremony, because when the candles flicker I see the red stripes that are cut into his back, fresh with blood that trickles down.

'Scourge the flesh to make the spirit strong,' Our Sister intones darkly.

She steps back into the circle and the two Sisters begin to attach him to the cross. His arms are tightly bound, ankles tied together and then they too are attached to the body of the cross. His head droops to one side, eyes barely open, mouth wet with spit that pours from his lips. Meek and submissive he's bound to his cross, crucified for the glory of his soul.

When he's firmly attached they begin to move the cross, trying to right it from the position on its side. For a moment I can't work it out, then I realise he's being hung upside down, head closest to the floor, feet where his head should be.

'Why's he upside down?' I whisper to the Sister nearest to me.

She looks at me sharply, as though I've committed some unforgivable sin. 'It would be obscene to crucify him in the manner of our Lord. The Apostle Peter was crucified like this,' she explains, casting a nervous glance towards Sister Catherine.

The cross is righted and somehow fixed in place. Now he's crucified upside down in a circle of fire, the flickering candle light making the sweat and blood that bathes him so glossy and sexy. There's blood all over, whip marks across his upper chest and along his thighs. He's out of his head with pain and pleasure, streaking through the pain barriers the way Our Sister explained. Is he on his way out? The question hits me like a kick in the cunt. Is this it? Does this poor bastard get to meet his maker today?

Sister Sarah is passing something round. I wait excitedly until it's my turn, anxious to gain some understanding. I feel drunk, my head's spinning and everything feels like a dream. I can hardly breathe, the air's so thick with wax and incense. Sister Sarah looks right through me, she's out of it too. She's handing out needles, long and sharp, and I take mine with hands that tremble.

Once the needles are handed round the next part of the ceremony begins. One of the Sisters walks forward, she kneels down by the circle of candles and clears a way forward. She stands and then walks through the gap in the circle of light, stopping abruptly before our crucified sinner. She's carrying a candle and a needle, which she heats up in the flame. I watch, wide eyed and dizzy, as she then pushes the needle into his thigh. He screams, his agony filling the room as the needle goes deep into his body. A trickle of blood pours along the steel needle until it drips slowly to the ground. The Sister crosses herself piously before her victim, as though paying homage to an icon. The bitch can't take her eyes off him, she's fascinated by the way he suffers, blood pouring, face a picture of ecstatic agony. Reluctantly she returns to our circle, and her place is taken by the next Sister in turn.

One by one they take it in turns, piercing his body with burning needles, drawing blood that weakens him as he screams and struggles. His arms are bound tightly, I can see him trying to pull free, or else he writhes uncontrollably. The stone walls are impenetrable, he is here to die, his screams will never be heard. I can feel it in the room, the hysteria that's going to have these dirty slags creaming themselves in their religious fervour. Suffering in abstract is nothing, here it's real, here they can see and feel the death struggles, they can see the life slipping away. And it's good, isn't it? To die like this, to be sacrificed in the name of the Lord.

Needles protrude from his thighs, his chest, his face. Each Sister seeks some new place, seeking to draw blood from a new wound. Some of them take great delight in pressing down on needles already in place, opening the wounds more, letting him scream and shake and spit. His eyes are white, it would take a week's worth of cock sucking to buy the junk to get anyone this far gone. He's going to die in a haze of junked out bliss that comes from inside his own head. No wonder these bitches used to be burned to death singing joyously. Fucking martyrs, fucking stupid bastards, cunts.

It's my turn, I'm next in line. Our Sister waits, she wants to see her latest protégé at work. I step forward, my gown swishing along after me. I stop at the circle of candles and pick one up, fascinated by the way the light is playing games with the shadows. I take it with me, gripping the thick base tightly, as though it's a prick I'm going to wank for money. Up close to the sinner I can see the tracks the blood have formed, a map of veins and arteries scorched on the outside of his body. Sweat and blood, so fucking elemental. His head is limp, he might be dead but for the slight heave of his chest as he breathes and the occasional moan of pain or pleasure, I can't fucking tell the difference any more.

The cloth around his waist is loose, soaked through and stinking. I pull it away, let it fall to the floor. His cock's half erect, pointing downwards, wet where he's pissed himself. Has he come? He might have done, I bring the candle closer to get a better look and the molten wax pours down, burning my hand before falling into the dark mass of hair around his cock and balls. His cock moves, gets slightly harder. I do it again, let the wax pour directly onto his cock, burning him directly. Jesus, his cock's erect, a sweaty specimen caked with wax and blood. I burn him some more, holding the candle so that the pure molten wax pours down onto his balls, onto his glans.

He moans, eyes flicker open. I can't fucking believe it, half dead and he's turned on, too dead to fuck but that's what he's got going on in his head. I spit viciously between his legs and the spear the candle into his arsehole. He struggles in vain, trying to twist away from me. The base of the candle is thicker than his cock but I force it into his arsehole, fucking him with it. Now the wax is trickling down the length of the candle and onto his genitals. Let him burn, the flame is already cooking his thighs as he struggles.

I turn, aware that the Sisters are silent, watching me with horror on their faces. This isn't in the ceremony, I'm not supposed to do this. Sister Catherine is silent, unless she makes a move the others will stay in line. I don't fucking care any more. I feel like I'm in a nightmare and I can do what I want and it won't matter. It won't matter because nothing matters, ever.

I'm still holding my needle. He is pierced all over his body, his nipples, his thighs, his arms, his lips. Not his cock. For the first time in ages he finds the power to scream as the needle pierces his glans, going in one end and coming out the other. It's bloody, the wet warmth squirting all over my hands. His cock's harder. I take a needle out of his thigh, pulling it out quickly and then, before he's got time to recover, it goes into the base of his cock. Again. His cock's going to get it all. One by one, each needle removed from his body is pushed back into his cock. This is what he deserves, the motherfucking piece of shit.

His cock is a heaving mess of steel and blood and flesh. His erection bigger than ever, so big I want to ride it to extinction. His balls are pierced finally, needle sinking in with hardly a murmur of complaint from his parched lips. I touch his mouth when removing the needle from his lips and I see just how dry he is.

I turn to face my Sisters, watching with a mixture of horror, delight and fear. I turn back to my victim. It's time this fucker woke up. I lift my gown and press my cunt to his lips. The piss comes naturally, emptying amber jewels of it into his bloodied face. He sucks it down, an elixir, I give him life with my piss. Isn't this what he deserves? To take life even in shit and piss and blood. This is it, fucker, this is the best it gets, life is the only thing there is.

As he sucks up my piss I bend lower and take the needle from the glans of his prick and push it into one of his nipples. Now the tip of his cock is clear, covered in blood and seminal fluid but free of the forest of steel that protrudes from the rest of it. I put it to my mouth, lapping my tongue around this damaged organ. The last drops of my piss are being sucked clean from my cunt and now he's discovering the fluid that only cunt can produce.

It's my turn to sigh and moan. I'm being sucked beautifully, his tongue lapping at my clit before he goes deeper. I return the favour by sucking deliriously on his damaged cock. I can taste his blood and his piss but now I'm getting the taste of his come too. When I climax I sink my teeth into the tender flesh of his glans and then he spurts into my mouth, wave upon wave of thick, warm come.

I turn again to face my Sisters. I smile and the squirt out the come I've just captured on my tongue. It sprays out, a shower of spit and come, I spit it out with all my heart and it reaches across the circle of fire and into their faces. Bitch! Bitch! Bitch! They're waking up, just as their victim is waking up. His orgasm has broken the spell, the little death need not lead to the welcoming arms of a Lord too cruel to want us to live.

'O, Jesus I can face you now.' I cry ecstatically, the words of scripture becoming my own at last. 'I spit in your face, shit Christ. The pleasure of crucifixion, that exquisite pain on the cross and of martyrdom is ours too. You died not for our sins, shit Christ, but for your pleasure. Our pain, our suffering, you stole. Fucker. I will not forgive nor forget. Saviour. Saviour of shit. O Jesus. Why? Fucker. Why? I stand and spit in your face and piss down your throat, shit fucker. Why didn't you save me? Betrayer. False prophet. There is no limit to my hatred or to my scorn. Shit Christ. You disgust me!'

They are stunned for a moment and then they attack. Screaming harridans. A rain of blows and kicks, sharp scratches. Pain, pain, pain and then darkness.

NINE

A blast of current, white light, screaming agony behind eyes that see nothing. Strapped down, arsehole stretched tight over a something hard and phallic. Electric pain and I cannot scream, cannot struggle, cannot escape. And a voice, somewhere, somewhere.

'It means nothing. When the world is sweetness, then remind yourself: It means nothing'

Electric pain merges with burning wax that fills my cunt. Cunt lips open, molten wax that runs like liquid gold into the soft membranes of my cunt. So many hands, pulling, hurting. Needles covered in blood pulled from another body and plunged into my own. Screams, a voice that wants to bring the walls tumbling down. Is that me screaming like a whore? Is that me spitting blood and piss?

Eyes that stare into darkness. And then my mouth is open. I puke, explosively, spraying the walls with vomit streaked with all the shit I've been made to eat.

I'm gagging as the blackness fades and I start to wake. I struggle, try to free myself but my arms are tied behind my back. I gag at the cock that is pushing deep into the back of my throat. I'm shivering, naked body bathed in icy jewels of cold water. Hand wrapped tightly in my hair, pushing my head up and down this cock fucking my mouth. Hard cock but I'm helpless, I start to use my tongue, sucking it properly, teasing the underside of the glans as my lips close against the hardness. A satisfied grunt is all the thanks I get as the cock squirts wads of spunk in the back of my throat.

My head is freed and I turn away and spit out the spunk I should've swallowed. White lightning in the eyes and I'm sprawled across the face, lips bleeding and face burning where I've been hit. I moan, turn over and open my eyes for the first time. The cock I've been sucking, or rather the cock fucking my mouth while I was still unconscious, belongs to the giant standing over me. He's tall, fat, powerfully built and with the sort of face that tells you all you need to know.

'What's wrong, whore? Don't like the taste of spunk?' he sneers.

I spit blood on the ground before I answer. 'You've got to pay extra if you want me to swallow,' I tell him, trying desperately to summon the only energy I've got left.

He laughs. 'Still got some spirit left,' he remarks. 'That'll go, we can't have that here.'

'Where am I?' I ask, trying a blood stained smile in the hope that I can win me some mercy. He's got a cock, he likes to have it sucked, my mouth must be worth something to him. Shit, he can't be worse than bitch Sister and her house of pain.

He smiles again, but there's no warmth there in those blue eyes. 'This is the compound,' he tells me. 'This is the end of the line. Fuck up here and you'll end up as fertiliser. Understand? No fucking up.'

'I won't, I promise,' I assure him with an urgency that can't be faked. We're in a bare cell, no bed but straw on the ground, no window but a slit in the wall sheds a diagonal of light.

'I know you won't,' he tells me. 'No one fucks up here. You've had it easy so far, from now you discover what it is to be an animal. Understand?'

'Yes, sir.'

'Call me Master,' he tells me. 'I am the Judge, the only authority here. As far as you're concerned that's all you have to know.'

'Yes, Master,' I tell him, struggling to sit up on my backside. The iron warmth of blood in my mouth subsides. I don't even want to know why I'm being judged, I just want to do as I'm told. I'm not thinking. Not thinking of anything.

'That's good,' he smiles once more. 'Do you know what I value the most?'

'No, sir, Master.'

'Obedience. That's all I ask, that's not too much to ask for, is it?'

'No, Master,' I agree. 'And I'll be obedient, I promise.'

'I know you will, and I'll test that obedience, you know that too, don't you?'

'Yes, Master.'

'You don't like the taste of spunk,' he remembers, scratching his chin with fingers that can crush the life from me without even trying.

'I'm so sorry, Master, it won't happen again. I'll swallow like a good girl,' I promise, putting on my girly voice in the desperate hope that it pleases him.

He drags me to my feet, powerful arms pulling me up as though I'm nothing. With arms cuffed behind my back I'm careful not to fall over, the cell is so small I'd smash my face to bits. He leads and I follow naturally, bare feet on cold floor, hardly aware of the fact that I'm naked. There's a hopeless, desolate air about this place and I know it's because the Judge is telling the truth: this is the end.

My cell is only one of many, housed in small stone sheds, part of a much larger compound. In the distance I can see a grand house, and I can't tell whether that's where I have just come from or whether it's where the Judge lives. All around me I see people in chains, working like slaves, cleaning, making, doing. There are guards, dressed, like the Judge, in black leather uniform, shiny boots and carrying whips or batons. As a whore I'd expected prison, but never something like this. Fuck, this is it, a fucking concentration camp.

I'm led to another of the buildings, from the outside it looks like a stable. Once we're inside I see that my guess was almost right. Only instead of horses there are rows of men, strapped up in leather bridles in their stalls. Animals like me, only this lot seem like prize specimens, bodies fit and strong, washed down, looked after with pride. One of them is being washed, attended by two young females who lather him up and wash him down as though he is a prize pony.

'Some of my best animals,' the Judge explains proudly. He walks to one of the stalls and strokes one of the men, rubbing his hand down smoothly shaven thigh. 'They're strong little horses,' the Judge continues, toying with the man's prick so that it springs stiffly to attention. I look from the man's hard cock to the terror in his eyes, I see myself there, my fear reflected in him. 'There are fifteen here and another ten in the stable next door, all of them perfect specimens.'

'Yes, Master,' I agree meekly. He's toying with the man's prick in the same absent way you'd stroke a favourite pet.

'I want you to swallow every drop of spunk they've got,' he orders me. 'No spitting or wasting a drop, understand? I'll have one of the stable boys take you round, understand?'

'Yes, Master, I'll swallow every drop they can spunk into my mouth.'

He smiles indulgently. 'I know that of course, but it'll be interesting to see if you can keep it all down. Careful, mind, they're frisky creatures and they like to play games.'

With that warning still ringing in my ears my hands are released. The stable boy is as naked as I am, a scrawny lad barely out of his teens. He shows not an ounce of interest in me or my body, instead he guides me to the first stall and pushes me roughly down onto my knees.

The Judge is leaning against the wall, watching with a sick smile on his face. I edge forward and take the pony boy's limp dick into my mouth. I work my tongue around and around, teasing and playing but the bastard doesn't want to play, there is no way he wants to shoot into my mouth. I look up at him desperately, begging eyes searching for some ounce of humanity in his. I suck harder, wondering how far I have to go before his cock twitches to life. I half turn and see that the Judge is still waiting.

Desperately I turn round, offering my backside to the human pony. I see the flicker of a smile on the edge of his lips. I begin to play with myself, pressing my fingers into my pussy but he turns away, uninterested. I kiss his feet, grabbing his attention once more. This time I begin to fuck my fingers into my back hole, frigging my tight anal hole vigorously until I'm on the edge of coming. His cock is hard now and I seize it in my mouth eagerly, keeping my fingers frigging my rear hole. As I suck he watches, fascinated by my display until he shudders and I suck every drop of salty come into my mouth.

I turn to the Judge and open my mouth, showing him the pool of come on my tongue. He smiles, nods and I swallow it for him. Before I move to the next stall I suck the pony boy's now limp cock of the last few droplets of come, making sure that none of his precious fluid is wasted. I hate it, but I know that I'm going to have to learn to love the taste of spunk going down my throat.

The Judge loses interest after I've sucked off the next two human ponies. He wanders off without a word, leaving me with a cock in my mouth and a minion to make sure I do as commanded. I don't stop. My lips and tongue work harder, my head slides up and down the length of a firm cock. I can lose myself in it, I don't have to think, don't have to wonder, don't have to be anything but a wet mouth on a hard cock. I swallow his come, letting it slip down the back of my throat, sucking harder as I feel his prick throb its release.

With barely a glance at the man who's spunk is now sitting in my guts, I move on to the next cock, already twitching with anticipation. I look across the stable, see the endless row of stalls and imagine the endless line of cocks and the gallons of spunk I have to swallow.

◆

The Judge is sitting at the dinner table when I am led in to see him. He doesn't even look up to acknowledge my existence, instead he's concentrating on his food, a mountain of meat cooked raw so that it runs with fat and blood. I am pushed onto hands and knees almost immediately by one of his many servants, and then allowed to crawl along the plush carpet towards him. I was right about the grand house, this is where he lives, able to oversee his dominion, and the dining room is as grand as the house. The walls are lined with pictures, portraits done in oils, landscapes and pictures of animals. The heavy oak table has room for many, but he is the only person here, apart from the two naked girls who serve him.

I crawl submissively towards him, taking my place at the side of his chair like an obedient bitch. My stomach gurgles, I feel a little bit sick, swelled up as I am on a diet of spunk and nothing else. I can taste it in my mouth, it perfumes my every breath, but not a drop of it has touched my tits or cunt, every drop has gone straight down my throat. Where's my defiance now? Where's my spirit? Beaten and fucked out of me, there's none of it left, there's just me, naked and alone in this nightmare.

The Judge snaps his fingers and points down to me. One of the minions rushes out of the room immediately, returning moments later with a silver bowl which is put down beside me. I watch silently as the Judge cuts strips of meat from a bone, thick, juicy slices of roast, tender and cooked to perfection. His strong hands skilfully carve the meat and then he drops a bare bone into my bowl. My first impulse is to scream, to demand some of what he's having. Fuck it! It smells so good, I can almost taste it, I imagine it melting in my mouth. What would I get for doing that? The question fills me with fear, the answer looming in my mind is too horrible to contemplate.

The bone is meant for me. It's what you'd give a bitch, and that's what I am, only I'm a whore as well as a bitch so that makes me worse. I start to gnaw at the bone, searching for the scraps of dead animal, licking my lips and tonguing the oozing oil and blood that coats it. My hunger is ignited and I look wistfully at the plate that my master eats from, the scraps on that would keep me happy but I'm not allowed that. He carelessly tosses another bone into my bowl and I seize it eagerly, desperate for the nourishment that a diet of spunk can't provide.

'How many cocks did you suck?' the Judge asks lazily, pushing back his chair so that he can gaze at me sucking on scraps of bone.

I wipe my mouth with the back of my hand. 'As many as you asked me to, Master,' I reply, realising that I hadn't even kept score. It feels like I've got the seed of a hundred men sprouting in my belly.

He laughs. 'You hate swallowing spunk but you didn't even count how many cocks shit into your pretty little mouth,' he tells me, evidently happy with my performance. 'That shows willing. If you'd answered twenty seven it would have meant that you had the time and the inclination to count, I would have taken that as a sign of opposition. I don't want mere submission, understand? I want complete subjugation. If I could rip you head open and smear your brains in the courtyard I'd do it, so long as your body functioned again afterwards.'

'There's no need for that, Master,' I whisper, heart throbbing painfully, 'I am yours completely.'

'Submission is temporary, it's something that a lover gives to another while they play games. I want much more than that. Call it capitulation, acquiescence, surrender, anything you like. Whatever you call it, it is absolute and permanent, understand?'

'Yes, Master, I understand,' I tell him meekly. He is sitting comfortably, long legs stretched out under the table. He is master of all he surveys, he holds the power of life and death in his monstrous hands and I'm terrified that I'll do wrong and then... I always do wrong, it's my destiny, my one true vocation in life.

'That sounds so glib,' he decides, looking down at my cowering figure. 'Do you know what true subjugation means? The perimeters of the compound are patrolled by dogs, have you seen them yet? Beautiful beasts, absolutely vicious, they know nothing but obedience. If they attack then they maim or kill with the cleanliness and precision that has been bred into them over a dozen generations. They are without a doubt the most vicious animals I have ever seen, and yet they are cowed in my presence. Dogs are pack animals, do you understand? If the pack attacked me then I wouldn't last more than a few minutes, but I am their master and they would rather attack one of their own kind then disobey me.'

He pauses and I don't know whether to speak or not. One of the serving girls removes the plate, laden with uneaten food, and I watch it go too afraid to beg for the scraps he has left behind. 'I love my dogs,' he continues while the other serving girl pours him a glass of wine. 'I've trained them well. I train my slaves in the same manner, without mercy or pity, I break their will until the idea of defiance has been erased from their minds completely. Do you know how far someone will go? Do you have any idea what complete subjugation can do to a man?'

'No, Master,' I reply truthfully, dreading the answer.

'I love my dogs and the pack leaders especially are devoted to me. Such fine creatures, they hold sway over the other dogs with a ruthlessness patterned after my own. I like to treat these dogs well, they have qualities of cruelty that I find enviable. As a present I gave them one of my slaves,' he laughs at the recollection. 'He showed some signs of defiance but he was so beautiful I decided to spare his miserable little existence. Instead I gave him to one of the dogs, a fine animal called Lucifer. It was a joy to watch Lucifer put this stupid boy in his place, he didn't even need to bite, he just bared his teeth and the boy's defiance collapsed. I still like to watch the boy being fucked by Lucifer, I like the way the boy grovels on hands and knees sucking that doggy cock before taking it in his arse. Sometimes some of the other dogs are allowed to fuck him too, I've seen my little dog fucker take it in the mouth and the arse at the same time, with the other dogs snapping to take their turn. That's complete subjugation, to fuck with dogs because that is what your master desires.'

I remain silent, appalled by what I have heard but even more afraid that he might decide that's what her wants from me. And would I do it? Shit, I can't even think about it without feeling sick.

'Master,' I whimper, 'please, let me suck your cock. My belly is empty without your spunk inside it.'

The Judge laughs heartily. He takes a slug of wine and then laughs some more. 'Afraid of joining my little dog fucker are you? You'll see him, I want you to watch him being fucked by Lucifer. You'll see how much he adores Lucifer now, how he grovels and pouts like a bitch on heat when Lucifer decides to fuck one of his own species.'

I say nothing, certain that I'll be forced to fuck Lucifer too. What choice would I have? What is the alternative to complete subjugation? It's death, what else can it be?

'Suck my cock now, bitch,' the Judge commands. 'Do it well or I'll have you whipped and thrown to Lucifer.'

I suck his cock as though it's the fountain of life. I lavish kisses, caresses and love on his massive cock. My lips squeeze his tool like a tight little cunt, my tongue wraps round and round until he forces my head down. He holds back the more I try to make him come, and then, when he's ready he pumps violently, raping my mouth with his force. I swallow his come, just as I've swallowed pints of it during the day. Shit, I swear I'm even beginning to like the taste.

'Good,' he sighs, pushing me away violently. 'I want you to eat spunk every day, understand? My ponies need to be serviced every day, you'll suck their cocks and do it just as lovingly as you did mine. I want that belly of yours nice and round and full of spunk all the time. I won't have you fucked any other way. Some bitches don't like to be buttfucked, so that's where they get it, that's the only way they are allowed to be fucked. Other bitches want in the arse because that's where they get their pleasure, I make sure they get it in the cunt only. And you, you spat out come and I want it put back a thousandfold. Only in the mouth from now.'

'Yes, Master,' I tell him meekly.

He laughs. 'That goes for Lucifer too, if I ever have him fuck you it'll be in the mouth. Your belly can swim with dog spunk as well.'

He snaps his fingers and one of the girls jumps to attention. 'Get me one of the guards,' he tells her. 'You'll suck the cock of any guard that wants it tonight,' he says, smiling at me, 'and believe me they'll all want a nice little mouth like yours.'

'Yes, Master,' I agree.

A guard appears and I follow him out of the dining room. I'm hauled to my feet and the unsmiling guard cuffs my arms in front of me, snapping ice cold steel around my wrists. 'You can blow me first,' he hisses into my ear, 'but only after I've arse fucked one of the other slaves.'

Then I'm led away, back to my cell for the night. I can see the dark hours stretching forward, an endless parade of dirty pricks and acrid semen for me to feast on. I begin to cry silently, tears trailing down my face. Why didn't I stay behind? Why didn't I help despatch that bastard on the cross? Now there's not even a pretence of salvation.

TEN

I sleep sucking cock, eyes closed but my mouth moving automatically. No counting, no point. Cock after cock fills my mouth until my lips are sore and cracked and I can feel the come rising in my throat. Shit, if spunk could reach critical mass I would explode like a bomb and take most of the compound with me.

And while I sleep, sucking and swallowing, I am haunted by weird dreams, dreams so real they feel like memories. I was someone else, once. A whore, a cheap body who fucked for cheap money. And before that I was someone else, a person I can't even remember, with a name and a family and a life worth living. A life worth living, the idea of it is so alien that I don't even see the joke any more. My world turned upside down, and now I am this living meat, this corpse that breathes and moves, barely existing instead of living. This isn't what I want, but what do my wants mean to a universe half-crazed with hate and destruction?

It means nothing. In a car with a woman who's cock I suck with joy. Being pissed on by a man of medicine. Sticking my tongue into a holy woman's arsehole. Plunging red hot pins in a crucified sinner. Sucking cock while I dream. It means nothing.

The days blur, merge, coalesce into a reality that is worst than anything I have ever dreamed. Surrounded by the stench of defeat, a smell of shit and spunk that fills my lungs with puke so bitter I can't get it out. I see bodies burned and branded, flesh singed with white hot metal so that the skin bubbles and bursts like meat on a skewer. Open wounds are wanked into, semen splashing into a pulsating mass of nerves and tissue so that the victim writhes with horror and pain. Women feast on scarlet menstrual blood, sucking it from each other's cunts, swimming in it, blood pouring from cunts and mouths. Victims tied and fucked with fists, clubs, guns. A woman shrieks as she is fisted front and back, her cries silenced with a prick in the mouth and the threat of worse.

I am numb to it. I see it and it means nothing. There is no sympathy inside me, no fellow feeling, nothing. I exist solely to eat spunk, to suck on any cock that's thrust into my open, willing mouth. When I see suffering I turn away, wishing the bleating of the victim would stop. Fuck it, if it hurts that much then let them die rather than carry on screaming.

I feast on come, my day is spent on hands and knees sucking cock. I have been forced to wear a strap on cock, an obscene phallus that pokes proudly from between my thighs, as though all the spunk I've swallowed has turned my cunt into prick. And with this prick I fuck other victims, I rape a young boy, fucking him as hard as I can until he bleeds from his arsehole and his tears of agony fall to the ground as thickly as the come from his tortured prick. Money changes hands and I am casually beaten by the guards who have gambled and lost.

I sit chained to the floor a lot of the time, staring into nothing or lost in silent admiration of the clouds. There's nothing in my head any more, nothing in my veins but congealed semen. The Judge remembers me once in a while and I service his cock while he expounds on the nature of submission and subjugation, knowing that I am completely broken. He tells me about the dog fucker, but I hardly listen as I slide my mouth up and down his hard cock. All I want is a pat on the head, a sigh of pleasure to escape his lips, a sign that I please him because in this domain that's all that counts.

My morning begins with a dull diagonal of light on the wall, light that sneaks through a tiny slit that is my window on the world. My hair is matted with come, plaited with the straw I've been sleeping on. This is what it feels like to be an animal. Distant screams announce the dawn, piercing the silence with a cry of agony. Screams followed by silence. Shit, I feel like screaming too.

'Awake already?' a voice demands, slamming open the door. It's still pretty dark outside, a beam of light from a torch blinds me for a moment.

'I'm hungry,' I whimper feebly, backing into a corner and curling up like a child. I want the darkness, I want it to embrace me, to take me away from all of this.

'Let me fill you up,' the guard laughs, advancing menacingly in the darkness.

'Please... I've been sucking all night,' I complain, ready to weep again. There was a time when tears were unknown to me. Anger was my emotion once, defiance the truth at the core of my being. Now I weep silently for fear that my sobs will be punished.

'If you've been sucking cock all night then you should be good at it,' my guard tells me, with the kind of sick remorseless logic that is the mark of their superior humour. The Judge calls his dog Lucifer and they think that's clever, the utterly banal and the supremely sublime are no different in their twisted vision.

I take his cock and kiss it, tasting the sweat with the tip of my tongue. He makes me get on all fours, stroking my back with his

Pan Panziarka

hands while I go down on him. His fingers press into my cunt, making me moan softly. 'Don't you like this?' he asks, as though I should be slick with cunt juice for sucking his prick.

I say nothing, I can feel that he's close, the way he's pressing deeper into me and the soft sighs he tries to hide tell me all I need to know. He takes his torch and pushes the handle into my pussy, forcing it deep into my body. I gasp but he carries on, pushing it in and out slowly, a giant prick to fuck me with while I take sustenance from his cock.

He grunts like an animal and spurts his semen into my mouth, waves of it arcing into the back of my throat. When he sits up he's smiling broadly, moronic eyes shining with delight. 'Dirty whore,' he jeers, showing me the end of his torch, wet with my pussy juice.

'I'm hungry,' I complain plaintively, ignoring his jeers.

'But you just had something to eat,' he chides me, laughing. He steps out into the darkness and returns with a bowl of mush, which he throws to the ground, spilling the content onto the floor. 'Here's your breakfast, you ungrateful bitch.'

I eat greedily, hungry for something, anything, other than spunk. Tasteless vegetable mush but it fills the void, I eat it despite the taste of stale piss with which it's flavoured. The guard snorts his disgust and walks out, leaving me to eat like the animal I have become. When I finish I sit back, ready to puke it all back up as it reacts with the gut full of spunk I've swallowed.

I crawl to the door, left carelessly open, and peer out cautiously. If I wanted I could walk out, stride defiantly into the courtyard to find out exactly where I am and to scout out an escape. I don't. It's safer to peer outside, ready to rush back to my corner at the first sign of danger.

There's some activity but the sun's not really high enough in the sky for me to see very much. I see four of the human ponies at work, yoked up pairs, harnessed in leather like the real thing, pulling a wagon load of slaves. I stare first at the human ponies, half naked apart from heavy boots and leather strapping, muscles taut as they strain to pull the load. Then I stare at the cargo, dull dead eyes sitting in shaved skulls, dirty bodies clothed in rags. They are broken, there's nothing left of them but tired bodies and the instinct to survive.

I should be shocked, what I see is the worst fucking nightmare but it all seems so normal. A guard snaps a whip at a group of slaves and they cower, too terrified to resist, too frightened to even attempt to get away. This is ordinary. A big grey sky, clouds that sweep from the horizon and threaten to piss down on us. It's all so fucking ordinary. The breeze makes the hairs on my arms stand on end. I'm still breathing. I'm still alive. So fucking ordinary.

A guard collects me and I follow without question, head slightly bowed, a step behind him. I'm shown into the stable and I drop to my knees. There's a row of eager cocks waiting to be sucked. This is it now. This is what I do. It feels like this is what I've always done. It feels ordinary, normal, mundane.

◆

I'm only pulled out of the stable after I've sucked all the cocks I'm supposed to. I used to hate the taste of spunk but now I don't have the energy to gag, I just swallow it all and let it sit inside me. I can even taste the difference between the come from a guard and come from a slave.

I'm allowed to drink dirty water from a trough and then I follow a guard across the courtyard and towards a group of out-houses. The sky is starting to clear a bit, dull light filtering through as though there's a chance of sunshine. In the distance I can see the trees moving gently in the breeze, and beyond that a group of slaves working in a field watched by a couple of guards who lean against a wagon and enjoy a smoke.

I see the Judge before he sees me. He's laughing and joking with a number of guards but I don't see what's going on until I get close. I notice the holster around his waist and wonder why I didn't see it before. The voices of the guards are full of cruel pleasure, violence heightened by derision. When one of them moves out of line of sight I see what the focus of attention is. I guess it's the dog fucker even before I hear him called that by one of his tormentors.

The dog fucker is a slim young man, wiry build, strong arms, hair and body obviously unwashed. There is a circle of guards around him, jeering, taunting. I can't see clearly, but he's on hands and knees and fully naked. One of the guards is also on his knees, leather trousers open at the waist and it's obvious he's attempting to sodomise the dog fucker.

The Judge looks up, looks right through me and then returns to the show. I'm nothing, not even worth noticing. The voices are louder now, the tone more urgently vicious.

'What's wrong, boy,' the guard attempting to rape the dog fucker is shouting, 'have you forgotten what a human prick is like up your arse?'

'Maybe he's trying for puppies,' one of the other guards remarks, to laughter from the Judge.

'Don't that feel better than a doggy prick?' the rapist hisses, shoving himself so hard into the dog fucker's backside that they both fall forward.

There is silence for a few moments as the rapist grinds his cock back and forth into his victim's backside. When the rapist shoots his load he slaps his victim hard a few times with the back of his hand, until the dog fucker lies flat on the ground whimpering.

'He doesn't like man sized cocks any more,' the rapist complains to his friends. 'What he needs is a man sized fist to open him up a bit more.' The suggestion meets with general approval and my guts churn in fear and sympathy. The poor bastard in front of me can do nothing, he is lower than shit in their eyes, his suffering doesn't even register.

'No,' the Judge says, intervening to stop the rapist fisting the dog fucker. There's a stunned silence, I feel relief and surprise at the gesture. The guards say nothing, I can see that they're as shocked as I am. 'He's Lucifer's boy,' the Judge explains with a smile of compassion, 'I don't want him stretched too much. I want him to be nice and tight for my best dog.'

More laughter. I feel nothing. The part of me that's supposed to feel is dead. Part of me is dead. I am numb.

The Judge turns to me. 'In his place, what would you choose?' he asks me, motioning me forward. 'Would you choose to let dogs fuck you or to die? How far would you take this mania for life and survival?'

I step forward and look down at the pathetic creature on the floor. Tears blur my vision. Sweet Jesus fucking Christ. I begin to weep and wail, falling blindly to my knees and scrabbling forwards to hold the cowering, confused body before me. I am whispering his name, whispering his name as I rock his head in my arms.

Arms grab me and pull me way, punching me in the belly when I cling to the dog fucker for dear life.

'Bastards! Bastards! Bastards!' I scream hysterically, kicking and punching the air instinctively. A few more punches and I'm rolling around the floor, spitting blood, groaning, clutching my guts as wave after wave of hurt pulses through me. *I don't deserve this. I don't deserve any of it.*

'Very brave and very stupid,' the Judge declares, standing over me, gun in hand.

'It's my brother,' I gasp through the pain. I turn and look into Terry's eyes, seeking the look of recognition that is worth dying for.

'Is this true?' the Judge asks, speaking to me and not to Terry.

'Kill me, please, kill me,' I beg, unable to endure.

The Judge stands back, smiling. 'I shouldn't be surprised,' he remarks to the others. 'There's no denying genetics. We farm the lowest of the low, the biological mistakes of a world gone mad. Brother and sister were bound to turn up one day, I should have expected it. Well, dog fucker,' he says, turning to Terry, 'it looks like it's a family reunion for you.'

Terry whimpers, fear in his eyes and nothing more. Each time someone talks to him he winces and cowers, there's nothing left in his head but the biological mechanisms of survival.

'How long's it been since you've been with a woman?' the Judge asks, and his audience of uniformed guards snigger like school kids. 'It's been a long time, hasn't it? Lucifer won't even let you mate with his doggy bitches, will he? Well, guess what, this is one family reunion that I'm going to enjoy. I want you to fuck her for me. Now. Here.'

Terry doesn't understand, he makes no move, shows no signs of having understood anything. A couple of hard kicks in the guts make him get up on hands and knees again. He offers them his backside, pale buttocks marked with bruises and cuts. They laugh and one of them pushes him towards me.

'Kill me you bastard! Kill me!' I beg as I am forced on hands and knees.

I struggle in vain. Terry gets the picture, he crawls towards me, unable to believe his luck. My arsehole is spat at, thick green phlegm used to lubricate me. He mounts me, hard cock pressing between my arse cheeks as I struggle and attempt to get away. Tears obscure my vision. His cock goes in, pushing hard and ruthless into my arsehole. His hands clamp tightly against my hips and he starts to bang away, fucking me harder and harder as he grows more confident.

The Judge is laughing, enjoying himself. The guards are hooping and hollering like stupid kids. The clouds part and the sun shines, rays of orange light falling across the two of us as my brother buggers me in public. I pant, moan, cry, come. Terry gasps, releasing hot jism deep inside me, fucking endlessly as though he never wants it to stop.

Terry sits back, laughing, empty eyes full of joy. One of the guards pats him on the head, the way they'd pat one of the dogs. The Judge unzips his fly and grabs me by the hair. I have cock to suck, that's what I'm here for.

♦

It feels so ordinary. That's what makes people so fucking evil. We make things ordinary, we make things normal. That's why concentration camps cook Jews, that's why people starve, that's why wars succeed. Horror piled upon horror piled upon horror, but we adapt, we accept. There's something lacking inside our shit brains, there's something wrong that makes us just carry on in the face of evil.

Selling cunt on the street. Normal. Slaving for a pittance. Normal.

Taking shit from people you hate. Normal. Being trapped in a life you hate. Normal. We accept what's unacceptable because we close our eyes to it. Horror and death, misery and failure, that's what life is. And this universe that actively hates us turns the screws by making us accept it all. That's it. Normal.

I dread the dawn, I dread opening my eyes and seeing that another day is here. But then something in my head filters out the shit and I carry on. I carry on because this is what my life is. The holocaust must have been like this, the nightmare transformed into a weird normality. Victims who are broken, who cling to life because that's all they have. Guards who laugh and joke as they work, who lavish love and attention on their pets whilst stoking the oven flames. So much fucking shit that you can't really see it any more.

The Judge strides into the room, and Terry crawls in after him. Terry is smiling, he is happy in the way only someone who is already dead can be happy. 'See,' the Judge tells me, 'I told you he couldn't wait to go back to Lucifer.'

'Yes, Judge, you're right,' I agree. I can smell canine on my brother's body, no doubt I'll see the doggy come leaking from his arsehole too.

'I want you to see Lucifer too,' the Judge tells me. 'It's time he had two people to play with, he's a good dog. You know,' he adds, 'I love my dogs completely. Do you know that if anyone dared to harm my animals I'd slaughter everyone in the compound? People like you are worthless, biologically irrelevant, genetic garbage, but Lucifer is different.'

He loves his dogs, he genuinely adores them. He's telling the truth, the only truth that matters. When his dog dies he's going to burn us all and weep for the loss of his friend. He'll hate the universe just the way I do, he'll curse the creation that put life on the world in order to take it back. But in the mean time we can suffer because we mean nothing to him and to his kind.

He yawns expansively and then walks over to my corner and releases the catch that has kept me in bondage for the last few hours. My body protests, shooting pains flaring through my tired limbs. I am honoured, a pampered pet though not quite on the canine level. Brother and sister, Terry and I share our Master's chamber and perform on command. My brother fucks me, or I fuck him, or suck him or we both suck our Master. Obedient and well trained, we survive while we entertain, knowing that when boredom sets in our lives will be worth less than that of the beasts in the fields.

The Judge yawns again and then walks back to his bed. He undresses slowly, stripping his leather uniform to stand naked before us, his drooping cock waiting to be coaxed to life. He looks at me and then at Terry, pondering the choice. He points at Terry, who smiles proudly, as though it is an honour to be chosen.

I crawl along the plush carpet while Terry lies on the bed, beside his Master. He begins to suck the Judge's cock, expertly taking the limp flesh and making it harder. I know that the moment I put my own lips to my brother's cock the Judge's cock will finally be stone hard.

We move seamlessly, mouths working in harmony so that our Master might find pleasure. I know what a delight it is for him to witness the sickest acts of incest, that the more extreme the act the greater his delight. To see me piss into my brother's mouth is a pleasure equalled only by seeing us share that piss in a passionate kiss immediately afterwards. I remember the paroxysms of delight while he watched me bugger fuck my brother while wearing a strap on cock, or the pleasure gained from watching Terry suck the semen he had spurted into my arsehole.

I move quickly, one moment sucking Terry's hard cock, trying to blot out the sharp canine smell imparted by his previous lover, the next moment I am on my feet. The gun is heavy and unfamiliar in my hand, but I know how to hold it, and it's aimed directly at the Judge's head. Justice has become lazy, or else the spark of defiance inside me was so faint that we were both convinced it had been extinguished forever.

He smiles, sighs softly while Terry continues to suck him. 'You'll never live,' he tells me, careful not to disturb Terry. His eyes betray not the slightest doubt, his smile supremely confident.

I nod. 'It means fuck all,' I whisper. 'Life is shit but there's nothing else. The universe hates us, it despises us with a passion that makes me want to weep... Don't we suffer enough just by being born? Don't we hurt enough when we spring bloodied and bruised from the womb? Why make it worse? Why hurt each other even more?'

Terry is moving sinuously, oblivious to everything but the bulging cock that he worships with his mouth.

'You talk like the whore that you are,' the Judge replies, breathing hard as he fights to prolong the pleasure. 'Accept things as they are... Death destroys all ideals, all utopias, every hope... What can you do against death?' There's still no fear in his eyes, there's nothing but pleasure at having his cock sucked beautifully by my brother.

'Look at the horror...' I whisper, speaking to myself. 'Fuck... We are surrounded by it, surrounded by more horror than we can bear to take. But I don't want to look away any more... I want to face it. I don't want to give up in the face of the universe. I won't accept it...'

'How you've grown...' the Judge sighs, closing his eyes as he teeters on the edge of orgasm.

The blast pushes me backwards, the gun exploding upwards. Terry gags as the come spurts thickly into his welcoming mouth. Blood spurting like come from the wound where the Judge's neck used to be. What has been a face looks at me, eyes filled with ecstasy that are slowly going out. He is released. Life giving seed pumping as his life gives way, as though in some awful way life will blossom again in the pit of my brother's stomach. I look at him, at the corpse that was all powerful, and don't know whether to feel envy, pity or vicious satisfaction.

The gun is still in my hand, cold steel resonating from the blast. There is no escape. The compound is the only reality, the world as it is not as it might be. But fuck it. This is it. Don't turn away, don't ever turn away.

I have to fight the horror.

THE LUSTS OF THE LIBERTINES
The Marquis De Sade

The Circle of Manias, the Circle of Excrement, the Circle of Blood; three gateways to a living Hell envisaged by the Marquis de Sade as he simmered in the bowels of the Bastille. An infernal zone where Libertines are free to pursue and execute their every caprice, no matter how depraved or inhuman.

Here, in a brand new, unexpurgated and explicit translation, are the 447 "complex, criminal and murderous lusts" of the Libertines as documented by de Sade in his accursed atrocity bible *The 120 Days Of Sodom;* a catalogue of debaucheries, cruelties and pathological perversions still unequalled in the annals of transgressive literature.

DUNGEON EVIDENCE: *Correct Sadist II*
Terence Sellers

The Mistress Angel Stern presides without mercy over a New York dungeon where her slaves, the "morally insane" of modern society, obey her every whim and undergo any degradation she wills upon them.

In the closed confines of a torture zone, these paraphiliacs and sexual malcontents use her image as an object for their masturbatory depravities, craving her cruelty in an abyss of sadomasochism and bondage.

Here are the bizarre case histories, philosophies and psychopathologies of a dominatrix; a frank testament which reveals not only the drives which lead some to become slaves, but also the complex exchange of psychic energies involved in scenes of dominance and submission.

THE VELVET UNDERGROUND
Michael Leigh

Swingers and swappers, strippers and streetwalkers, sadists, masochists, and sexual mavericks of every persuasion; all are documented in this legendary exposé of the diseased underbelly of '60s American society.

The Velvet Underground is the ground-breaking sexological study that lent its name to the seminal New York rock'n'roll group, whose songs were to mirror its themes of depravity and social malaise.

Welcome to the sexual twilight zone, where the death orgies of Altamont and Helter Skelter are just a bull-whip's kiss away.

velvet

SISTER MIDNIGHT *Jeremy Reed*

The Marquis de Sade is dead – but his sister is alive and well, stalking the ruins of the château of La Coste where she reconstructs the apocalyptic orgies, tortures and blasphemies of her brother's reviled last will and testament, *The 120 Days Of Sodom.*

Castle freaks, killing gardens, lesbian love trysts on human furniture; these and countless other configurations of debauched carnality conspire and collude in a sundered, dream-like zone where the clock strikes eternal midnight.

Sister Midnight is the sequel to Jeremy Reed's erotic classic *The Pleasure Château,* a continued exploration of decadent extremes and sexual delirium in the tradition of de Sade, Sacher-Masoch and Apollinaire; a tribute to undying lust and the endless scope of human perversion.

THE SNAKE *Melanie Desmoulins*

When Lucy, a sexually frustrated young widow, is mysteriously sent a plane ticket to Portugal, she takes a flight into erotic abandon which can only lead to death and damnation.

Soon seduced by both a debauched Englishwoman and her Portuguese husband, she sheds the skin of morality like a snake and begins to act out her darkest, uninhibited sexual desires. Increasingly depraved rituals of narcotics abuse, Satanism and sadomasochism – presided over by Bartolomeo, a Sade-like albino cult leader – eventually lead to the total disintegration of Lucy's ego.

At Bartolomeo's isolated villa, a shrine to pornographic art and literature, she finally enters the snake pit...

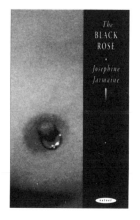

THE BLACK ROSE *Josephine Jarmaine*

Abducted to a mysterious French island, sixteen-year-old Rosamund finds herself at the mercy of the Duke and his four libidinous sons. She soon learns that her virginity must be sacrificed in order to breed the Black Rose, a rare flower whose aphrodisiac elixir will transform the world into a polysexual playground of orgiastic and orgasmic excess.

Rosamund's carnal initiation plunges her into a vortex of pain and pleasure, as she discovers that the Château Rose is a sensory realm where sadism, sapphism, sodomy, incest, bestiality, bondage and rampant fornication are a way of life.

The Black Rose is a stunning hybrid of decadence and explicit sexuality, a unique modern classic.

VELVET PUBLICATIONS

PHILOSOPHY IN THE BOUDOIR *The Marquis de Sade*

In the boudoir of a sequestered country house, a young virgin is ruthlessly schooled in evil. Indoctrinated by her amoral tutors in the ways of sexual perversion, fornication, murder, incest, atheism and complete self-gratification, she takes part with growing abandon in a series of violent erotic orgies which culminates with the flagellation and torture of her own mother – her final act of liberation.

Philosophy In The Boudoir is the most concise, representative text out of all the Marquis de Sade's works, containing his notorious doctrine of libertinage expounded in full, coupled with liberal doses of savage, unbridled eroticism, cruelty and violent sexuality. The renegade philosophies put forward here would later rank amongst the main cornerstones of André Breton's Surrealist manifesto.

THE SHE-DEVILS *Pierre Louÿs*

A mother and her three daughters...sharing their inexhaustible sexual favours between the same young man, each other, and anyone else who enters their web of depravity. From a chance encounter on the stairway with a voluptuous young girl, the narrator is drawn to become the plaything of four rapacious females, experiencing them all in various combinations of increasingly wild debauchery, until they one day vanish as mysteriously as they had appeared.

Described by Susan Sontag as one of the few works of the erotic imagination to deserve true literary status, *The She Devils (Trois Filles De Leur Mère)* remains Pierre Louÿs' most intense, claustrophobic work; a study of sexual obsession and mono-mania unsurpassed in its depictions of carnal excess, unbridled lust and limitless perversity.

THE PLEASURE CHATEAU *Jeremy Reed*

The story of Leanda, mistress of an opulent château, who tirelessly indulges her compulsion for sexual extremes, entertaining deviants, transsexuals and freaks in pursuit of the ultimate erotic experience. She is finally transported to a zone where sex transcends death, and existence becomes a never-ending orgy of the senses. The book also includes *Tales Of The Midget*, astonishing erotic adventures as related by a dwarf raconteur versed in decades of debauch.

Jeremy Reed, hailed as one of the greatest poets of his generation, has turned his exquisite imagination to producing this masterpiece of gothic erotica in the tradition of de Sade, Apollinaire and Sacher-Masoch, his tribute to the undying flame of human sexuality.

FLESH UNLIMITED *Guillaume Apollinaire*

The debauched aristocrat Mony Vibescu and a circle of fellow sybarites blaze a trail of uncontrollable lust, cruelty and depravity across the streets of Europe. A young man reminisces his sexual awakening at the hands of his aunt, his sister and their friends as he is irremediably corrupted in a season of carnal excess.

Flesh Unlimited is a compendium edition of *Les Onze Mille Verges* and *Les Mémoires d'Un Jeune Don Juan*, Apollinaire's two wild masterpieces of the explicit erotic imagination, works which compare with the best of the Marquis de Sade.

Presented in brand new translations by Alexis Lykiard (translator of Lautréamont's *Maldoror*), these are the original, complete and unexpurgated versions, with full introduction and notes.

INFORMATION

You have just read a *Velvet* book
Published by:
Velvet Publications
83, Clerkenwell Road, London EC1R 5AR
Tel: 0171-430-9878 Fax: 0171-242-5527
E-mail: velvet@pussycat.demon.co.uk

Velvet publications should be available in all proper
bookstores; please ask your local retailer to order from:

UK & Europe: Turnaround Distribution, Unit 3
Olympia Trading Estate, Coburg Road, Wood Green,
London N22 6TZ
Tel: 0181-829-3000 Fax: 0181-881-5088

Italy: Apeiron Editoria & Distribuzione
Pizza Orazio Moroni 4
00060 Sant'Oresta (Roma)
Tel: 0761-579670
Fax: 0761-579737

USA: Subterranean Company, Box 160, 265 South 5th
Street, Monroe, OR 97456
Tel: 541-847-5274 Fax: 541-847-6018

USA Non-booktrade: Xclusiv, 451 50th St, Brooklyn,
NY 11220
Tel: 718-439-1271 Fax: 718-439-1272
Last Gasp, 777 Florida St, San Francisco, CA 94110
Tel: 415-824-6636 Fax: 415-824-1836
AK Distribution, PO Box 40682, San Francisco,
CA 94140-0682
Tel: 415-864-0892 Fax: 415-864-0893

Canada: Marginal, Unit 102, 277 George Street, N.
Peterborough, Ontario K9J 3G9
Tel/Fax: 705-745-2326

Japan: Tuttle-Shokai, 21-13 Seki 1-Chome, Tama-ku,
Kawasaki, Kanagawa 214
Tel: 44-833-1924 Fax: 44-833-7559

A full catalogue is available on request.

ORDER FORM   *(please photocopy if you do not wish to cut up your book)*

TITLE *(please tick box)*	PRICE	QUANTITY	TITLE *(please tick box)*	PRICE	QUANTITY
☐ The Lusts Of The Libertines	£7.95		☐ Flesh Unlimited	£7.95	
☐ Dungeon Evidence	£9.95		☐ The Whip Angels	£4.95	
☐ The Velvet Underground	£7.95		☐ House Of Pain	£4.95	
☐ Whiplash Castle	£7.95		☐ Irene's Cunt	£7.95	
☐ The Snake	£7.95		☐ Psychopathia Sexualis	£9.95	
☐ The Black Rose	£7.95		☐ Torture Garden	£16.95	
☐ Philosophy In The Boudoir	£7.95		☐ Baby Doll	£12.95	
☐ The She Devils	£7.95		☐ City Of The Broken Dolls	£12.95	
☐ The Pleasure Château	£7.95		☐ Heat	£14.95	

Total Amount £_____   ☐ I enclose cheque/money order   ☐ I wish to pay by ☐ Visa ☐ Mastercard

Card No: |__|__|__|__|__|__|__|__|__|__|__|__|__|__|__|__| Expiry_____

Signature_____ Date_____

Name_____

Address_____

_____ Telephone_____

Please add 10% to total price for postage & packing in UK (max. £5.00) 20% outside UK (max £10.00).
*Make cheques/money orders payable to **Velvet Publications** and send to 83 Clerkenwell Road, London EC1R 5AR (Sterling only)*

VELVET PUBLICATIONS